SHADOW AND FLAME

Book III of the
Imperial Chronicles

Shadow and Flame

ISBN 978-1-958724-14-9

THE COMING YEARS WOULD TEST THE COURAGE
OF CITIZENS AND SUBJECT PEOPLES, OF
LEGIONARIES AND SLAVES, OF THE MEN AND
WOMEN OF THE EMPIRE; AND DETERMINE
WHETHER THE NATION CHOSEN BY IMPERIUM
WOULD FULFILL ITS CALLING: TO RULE OVER ALL
THE WORLD.

—Primo Alleus, national historian, writer of *The Imperial Chronicles*

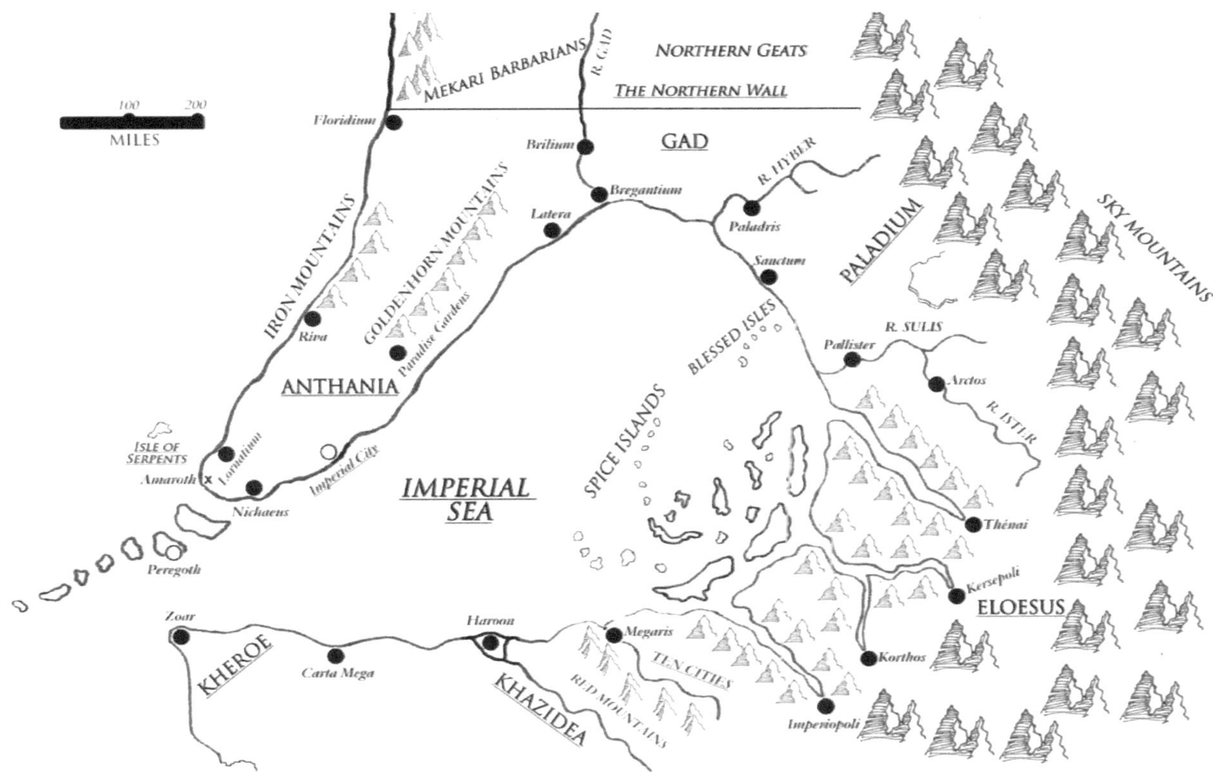

MILES
100
200
MEKARI BARBARIANS
R. GAD
NORTHERN GEATS
THE NORTHERN WALL
Floridium
Brilium
GAD
Bregantium
R. HYBER
Latera
Paladris
PALADIUM
SKY MOUNTAINS
IRON MOUNTAINS
GOLDENHORN MOUNTAINS
Riva
Paradise Gardens
Sanctum
ANTHANIA
BLESSED ISLES
R. SULIS
Pallister
Arctos
ISLE OF SERPENTS
Lornation
Imperial City
SPICE ISLANDS
R. ISTER
Amaroth
IMPERIAL SEA
Nichaeus
Thénai
Peregoth
Kersepoli
Zoar
Haroon
ELOESUS
KHEROE
Megaris
Carta Mega
TEN CITIES
Korthos
KHAZIDEA
RED MOUNTAINS
Imperiopoli

Imperial City

WARDS (LABELED)
a. Armory District
b. Kings Terrace
c. Maxima
d. Villa Regis
e. Bulus Wharf
f. Market District
g. Canyon Row
h. Newmarket
i. Mud Bottom
j. Meridia
k. Mystia
l. Villa Mares
m. Loud Surf
n. Perrine
o. Gaboline
p. West Limes
q. East Limes
r. Terrentian
s. Majorian Markets
t. The Strand
u. Meletus
v. Urubus

THE CITY: ITS SIGHTS AND WONDERS

City Bounds: *No legions may enter. It is the law.*
Wagontown Settlement: *A Haunt of Halflings.*
Dualmis: *An island across the sea.*
Imperial Harbor: *A wonder of the world.*
1. Imperial Square: *The Imperial Palace, the Council House and the Hippodrome, among other wonders.*
2. Campus: *The city's most ancient boundary.*
3. Imperial Arena: *Glory. Honor. Blood.*
4. Walk of Triumph: *See the nation's heroes and be amazed.*

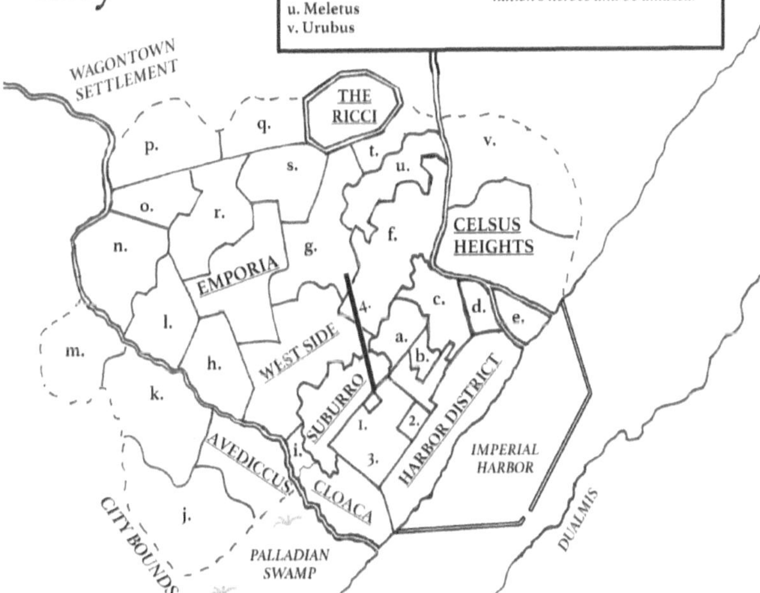

PROLOGUE:
THE DESOLATION

Alesso Komenos, Legate

Through the cracked, fire-hardened hell of the Desolation, in the wavering sun-scorched air, a dense crowd took shape through the veil of haze. The instructions of Emperor Severus could not have been clearer: Kill everything that shows its face.

But from Alesso's vantage point on the balcony of Fort Tidus, curiosity grew in his mind. It was a weakness of his, he supposed. The crowd was certainly not an army; they did not walk like one, nor were there the cataphracts or heavy infantry that made the southron armies famous. No, these were civilians. Peasants, perhaps.

He turned and there, as he expected, stood Mather Varis, the second-in-command. "Come with me," Alesso told him.

Into the hot sun Alesso walked, across the scorched hardpan earth the Empire had burned and sown with salt more times than he could remember. The air wavered before him, and the standard-issue breastplate drained his strength in the heat. He so rarely left the cool air of the fort.

As he drew closer, there was no mistaking the wretched forms before them. Fharese peasants from beyond the Desolation, likely hungry judging by their gaunt faces, and likely weak judging by their slow movements. *Refugees*, Alesso realized. *And they must be truly desperate to beg shelter from their foe.* Alesso often wondered why the padisha no longer sent armies to wage war on them. *There is trouble in the South*, he realized. It was the only explanation.

When they reached Alesso and Mather, an old woman at the front of the crowd let out a wail and fell down face-first, weeping. An old man—her husband, perhaps—knelt to the ground and knit his fingers together. "Please, northern masters! We have nowhere to go! We have nothing to eat! We will sell ourselves as slaves if need be!"

Slaves. Alesso frowned. *I could profit from their misery.* The legion had turned him cold.

"The nomads drove us from our home!" another, younger man at the front of the crowd shouted through a thick accent. "They killed most of us."

Nomads. These were southrons, Alesso reminded himself. These people were the enemy. Emperor Severus said to give no quarter. And Alesso prided himself on his dutifulness, never questioning the commands of Severus, the Hand of Imperium, the emperor that Claudian Adamantus had personally appointed. The god Imperium smiled on Severus. Who was Alesso to argue with his lord's commands? He knew what he had to do.

"Tribune, bring a hundred legionaries," he told Mather Varis.

Varis quickly turned and left.

Alesso could barely meet the peasants' eyes. He had taken oaths to serve the people of the Empire, the lord emperor and the august Imperial Council. He was not here to appease the southrons. He reminded himself of this over and over, lest his welling compassion get the best of him.

He tossed a furtive glance back. Mather Varis had become a speck in the distance.

~

At last the soldiers' stamping ironshod feet reached them. Alesso looked back. The men, in their thin steel breastplates and giant horsehair-crested helmets, bore the red-gold shields of the Imperial Army and swords that would soon drip with blood. They had been trained to obey without resistance, to serve their lord legate and the Empire itself.

He turned his gaze back to the gray-garbed crowd before him. He bit his lip so hard it began to ache.

The old woman looked up at him from her prostrate position. "Imperial masters," she wept, "the nomads came from the east. The Dark Horde has poured out from the desert lands. They have destroyed the shrines of Atman and Athra. Not even the magi can stop them. I beg you, Imperial masters, please…"

The legionaries closed in on them. Alesso held up his hand and they stopped. "The Dark Horde, you say."

"They demand fealty to their lord Mazda. They came from the desert far to the east," the woman continued in a strained voice. "These people who had nothing, who were no concern of the King of Kings, who lived—year by year and age by age—in the barren sands… they have poured out following the Silk Route, and the Horse Peoples fight with them. I beg of you, Imperial. We will be glad to live our lives in slavery, as long as we do not live under the Dark Horde."

Alesso's teeth nearly drew blood. At last, he spoke. "Leave the women and children alive."

The legion rushed in and a slaughter followed. Heads rolled, innards flew, and blood soaked the hardpan soil like it had so many times before. The peasants took their punishment silently.

They have given up. "Take the women and children to Haroon." Each word was a struggle. "Sell them to good masters, Mather."

Mather Varis nodded. Alesso turned and walked back in the direction of Fort Tidus. The news from the Southern World could not be ignored. They were the enemy, yes, and they had been since the beginning. But he wondered if the enemy of Fharas—the Dark Horde—was the Empire's friend, or a foe worse than Fharas had ever been.

Alesso felt dirty after what had gone on. He would have to write the emperor and send the message with Mather. But the old woman's eyes haunted him, those eyes glazed with tears. *What have I done,* he asked himself. *What have I done?*

Duty, he told himself, and thought of it no more.

1091

CHAPTER ONE:
NEWS FROM THE SOUTH

Tiverio Lucullus, Maestro of Foreign Affairs

Everything changed when the emperor sat on the White Throne. People treated Bathalomer Severus like the feeble, white-haired man he was he left it, and like a god when he took the seat that Claudian had given him. Sometimes, Lucullus wondered how things would be different if Claudian had remained emperor.

He also wondered if Bathalomer could read his mind. It would not surprise him if the rumors were true, that he had the gift of magic.

The doors to the White Chamber opened a crack. Hieron, Marshal of the Imperial Guard, strode in and his red half-cloak fluttered behind him. He knelt to the ground and gazed up at Emperor Severus.

"Your Undying Glory," he began, "a man named Mather Varis requests an audience with you."

"A Paladian name." A hint of a smile touched Bathalomer's wrinkled face, but only a hint. It vanished in an instant. "Who is he?"

"A tribune of the Second Harak Legion. He brings a report of the Desolation."

"A report," Bathalomer intoned. "Surely it is not something to bother my Undying Glory about." The hint of a smile returned. "Send him in."

Lucullus drew back into the shadows.

Mather Varis was short for a Paladian, but every bit of him was muscle. His blue eyes had the self-assurance of a man who'd spent his life in the camps, and when he knelt before the Emperor Severus and spoke, his voice did not quiver. "Your Undying Glory," he said, "there is trouble in the South."

"In the Southern World," Emperor Severus said, "or in the south of our nation? If the southrons have trouble it is not our concern. In fact, it is good for us."

"Good for us." Mather did not sound as certain. "There are refugees coming, sometimes more than once a week. Your express orders were to kill anyone who comes. Your legate Alesso has obeyed this strictly, for the most part. Many wish to be slaves, but Alesso is honorable to his oaths."

Bathalomer frowned. "He has taken my orders too literally, Mather Varis." He spoke the name as if Mather were the stupidest man in Varda. "A slave is far more profitable than a corpse."

Lucullus stayed in the shadows, watching everything unfold quietly though he did not fear Bathalomer. The emperor had vices like everyone, but anger was not one of them.

"Indeed," Mather Varis said. "I shall tell him. But there is more."

"Go on, then."

"The trouble in the South… the King of Kings is embroiled in a war with nomads. I do not think we have much to fear from the southrons. But I do wonder if we should help them."

"*Help them*?" Emperor Severus' patience had evaporated. "Ah, Mather, what is wrong with you? We are their enemies. Did the King of Kings help us in our troubles with the north? When the barbarians nearly burned down Bregantium, were there cataphracts and war-elephants to save us?"

"But if the nomads overcome them, overtake Taifun… they may turn their focus on us."

Taifun. A city far from the Empire in distance, and even further in mind. Lucullus wondered what the emperor would decide.

"Nomads." Severus' frown deepened. "The name does not exactly strike terror into my heart. Does it strike fear into yours?"

Mather Varis' expression remained strong and somber, but he said no more of it, perhaps realizing he could not win this fight. "There is another rumor… perhaps you remember from your history lessons.

Nearly a hundred years ago, a brother-sister monarchy ruled Haroon. Anakh the Brother-King, and Astarthe the Sister-Queen. Do you recall?"

Severus' already-pasty face paled further. "Yes. Claudio the Divine put an end to them."

"That is what we all thought," Mather Varis went on. "But it seems they have living descendants. Anakh and Astarthe are in the city of Saidoon under the protection of the Tiger Queen. They have a claim to the Red Throne of Haroon, or at least they think they do."

"And with the South in trouble they'd have little chance of taking it back." Yet Lucullus had grown to know Bathalomer Severus, and his tone indicated he worried more than he let on.

"Indeed," Mather Varis said. "It is a small concern."

"They would not dare," Emperor Severus began. "We shall not concern ourselves with it."

But Lucullus knew he would.

CHAPTER TWO:
BROTHER SISTER, KING AND QUEEN

Astarthe

Of all the places she, her brother, and their protector Issachar lived, Astarthe hated Saidoon the most. Even in the lightest clothing, Astarthe couldn't escape the awful heat. She would take a bath in the communal pools and go to bed, and when she woke up she was covered in sweat again. Her brother Anakh didn't like it here, either. Anakh said it was because of the heat, but Astarthe thought what he really didn't like were the tigers—which the queen let wander around the city as if they were dogs or cats—but Anakh would never admit it because he wanted to seem tough. And when it was just Astarthe and the Godling priest Issachar, it was nice to have someone who was tough, or at least tried to be.

Issachar made it clear that one day Astarthe and her brother would have to marry. Even though she liked her brother and got along with him the best of anyone, and even though his hair had started to bud on his face and chest and other places, she couldn't help but think it wasn't right. Astarthe loved her brother but not like that. When Astarthe told their protector Issachar, he would snap at her. He would say that it is the way it has always been. The Queen of Haroon would marry her brother, and Astarthe would do it just like all her ancestors had. And Astarthe, deep down, knew that eventually she would have to. Issachar had struck her before, and when his eyes bulged and he began to shout Astarthe would do anything to stop it. Issachar said that one day, she and her brother would be one. And day by day, Astarthe began to realize that she would have to. Her brother would be her husband, as it had been since the beginning. Because of it, the blood of the Sun God and the Moon Goddess ran pure to the last generation. Issachar said that Astarthe was the vicar of Issa, the Moon embodied; and that Anakh her brother was the vicar of Atman, the

Sun embodied.

As Astarthe stood there, looking out the window to the communal pools, a cool draft indicated the door behind her had opened. When she turned to look back, the lanky figure of Issachar. He wore a woman's robe like all the priests of Atman did, and from a distance no one could tell whether Issachar was a man or not. When it happened, Astarthe laughed. Issachar didn't like it when she laughed about that. He didn't like it when she laughed at all.

"Astarthe." Issachar had a trace of anger to his voice, and a trace of anger in his eyes, but Astarthe could tell it was not directed at her. It was something else. The Tiger Queen. "The Tiger Queen," he confirmed, "wishes to speak with us. Get ready. We must be careful, Astarthe. Remember when she impaled the Surese emissaries for the looks they gave her?"

"Yes." Astathe gulped. She started to undress. Issachar gave one last look, and shut the door.

~

The Tiger Throne of Saidoon was a hundred yards outside the ziggurats and shanty homes of the city. The giant stone edifice lay in the middle of the jungle, and the Tiger Queen sat on it nearly all the time, even now in the midday heat. Her consorts sat all around her, both men and women, having the same features she did: gray-brown skin, frizzy silver hair, and large brown eyes. She rose from her too-large throne, grabbed her beaded spear, and slammed the hilt onto the stone.

The consorts jerked to their feet. In the distance, drummers pounded out a ceremonial beat. Astarthe knew what to do: fall to her knees. Issachar was kneeling by the time she was; Anakh, as always, was a half a second late. *Always trying to out-man people.* She smiled. She liked his courage but it might get him killed someday.

"Words from the Queen Ninchan."

"We hear and obey," the trio said in unison.

"A man from far north, a whiteskin merchant, has been visiting the Spice Cities and asking many questions. They involve you." Ninchan had an angry look to her eyes, and it scared Astarthe even more than Issachar. "When I said you could stay, you said you would bring no trouble. You said you would stay with us, keep to yourself. But it seems the northerners want you, Issachar. If the whiteskins pay, the King of Kings will come here and give us trouble. We do not want any trouble, Issachar. You told me to not say a word and I honored my oath. The King of Kings has burned his subjects alive for less."

"Tiger Queen Ninchan." Even in the direness of the situation, Issachar's voice had an arrogance to it. Astarthe smiled at that. "The King of Kings has enough trouble already to worry about us. The nomads have reached the walls of Taifun how many times now? The pashas of Sur have broken free of his control. The Sea Raiders will not come to his aid. Do you really think he cares about a little boy and a little girl?"

"Silence!" Ninchan hissed. "You will not talk to the Tiger God's daughter that way. The Mother Flower is always hungry, and she does not care whether the meat is male or female, or something in-between."

A few of Ninchan's consorts giggled. Astarthe had no doubts Issachar wanted to kill Ninchan right then and there, but even in his wrath he was not stupid. Issachar was the wisest man Astarthe ever knew, except for maybe Anakh.

She looked at her brother from her kneeling position. He had that look to his eyes, that flush to his cheeks; he was just as angry as Issachar. Astarthe thought better of getting angry at the Tiger Queen. Besides, it wasn't the fire of anger she felt; it was a coldness in her gut, a clamminess to her hands. Her brother and her protector were angry, she could feel it; but Astarthe was afraid.

The Tiger Queen was not lying about the Mother Flower threat. Whenever a murderer or a thief or a deviant was caught, she would throw them into one of the Mother Flower's pitchers, deep in the jungle. The Mother Flower liked them dead, so when Astarthe felt the presence of a few dozen behind her—warriors, judging by their violent thoughts—she realized what was coming before the Tiger Queen spoke.

"It is best that you never existed, Issachar. It is best for me, and maybe it is best for you."

Together, they glanced back. Thirty warriors, naked and smeared with blue war-paint, approached with spears. The fire of anger had left Issachar's eyes, melting down into panic. Astarthe could feel his terror building up. She had no doubts his heart was racing.

"I am sorry it has come to this!" the Tiger Queen shouted.

The warriors charged. Astarthe looked back. "Wait!" she cried, and let loose what Issachar had told her not to—the *gleaming,* the power she'd always had—and felt, in an instant, the Tiger Queen's change of heart. She was transfixed now, a pawn—as Issachar explained—and she could suggest things to the Tiger Queen. "Let us stay!" she said at first. "No… let us go. You can give us a ship. You can send us away. It would be in your best interest, O Tiger Queen." And with that release of the *gleaming,* all energy left her. She nearly collapsed, panting. That was how it always worked. She could only touch that part of her soul so long before she could do no more. Issachar had told her to never use her *gleaming* ever again, but she had hopes he would see it differently, now.

"Yes, yes," the Tiger Queen purred. "Stop, warriors! We will send them on a ship. To Sur, perhaps, to Janshi… or to the Spice Cities… or the Dark Land."

Astarthe shuddered. Molkoro, the so-called Dark Land, was a horrid place, a godless place. "Not the Dark Land."

When she looked back, the queen's warriors had lowered their spears.

"Pack your things," the Tiger Queen snapped. Some of the charm had worn off. "Hurry. Do not waste the time."

"We hear and obey," Astarthe, Anakh, and Issachar said in unison, and turned to leave. The warriors parted at their coming.

Anakh

As Anakh put all his meager things into a sack, the beating echoed through the door. His sister, his soon-to-be wife, sobbed: "I'm sorry! I'm sorry!"

And Issachar, their cruel Godling master, was hissing at her: "I told you to never use the *gleaming!* You knew that would make me angry. You deserve this."

"I'm sorry! I'm sorry!"

Anakh began to undress. He would put on a new set of clothes for the journey. *I am a man.* Black hair had begun to grow on his chest. Soon he'd be strong enough to overpower Issachar and give him the beating of his life. He couldn't wait until the day. *But it is not now.*

Astarthe cried out again.

It is not now, Anakh told himself, and tried to quell his anger to no avail.

CHAPTER THREE:
THE GROWING DARK

Pyoter Matheris, Hunter

The sun set over the moors of North Paladium. The heat of the day faded like a wilting flower. The cool set in, but Pyoter was not naïve enough to think it caused his goosebumps. A howl pierced the uneasy silence. Pyoter had no doubts it was what the local called the "black dog" of the moors. Some demonologists thought it was mere misunderstanding, that a legend had developed out of a pack of stray dogs, in a society already gripped by paranoia and fear. Pyoter knew better. He called the black dogs of the moor hellhounds, and they appeared where a cabal of demoniacs was at work. They appeared when bad things happened.

Pyoter fingered his crossbow. He was alone on the causeway as it wound its way through the marsh. Demoniacs did not like to do their dirty work in the open. Though things unthinkable to their grandfathers now happened openly and brazenly in the full light of day, most citizens of the Empire still had the decency to despise demoniacs, excute the ones they knew—with or without a trial—and decry them publicly. Though the gods' enemies found favor in the hearts of the lunatics, the hopeless and the wretched, demoniacs were few in number—and it was Pyoter's mission to eliminate them altogether. As a sworn brother of the order of Hunters, it was his duty. And it was also his heart's desire.

He turned down a fork in the causeway. The town proper lay a mile away. Varister was the largest settlement in the region, but still a flyspeck village compared to Sanctum or the other great cities of the Empire. Yet the demoniacs had gained a great foothold here, and it was Pyoter's mission to destroy it.

A chill wind gusted over him, nearly knocking off his wide-brimmed hat. Another moor dog howled, then another seconds later.

I have lost the trail. I don't know where they are. His fingers fidgeted dangerously on the crossbow lever. He turned and looked around. All that greeted him were bulrushes, sedges and the glint of water in the moonlight.

He drew in a deep breath. *Hieronus guide me,* he prayed. But all that greeted him was silence and the stagnant moonlit waters.

An uncertain hour passed. The moon hung bright overhead, white and full. He had turned down more forks in the causeway than he could possibly remember. More silence was his reward. Silence, and the howls of moor dogs.

And drums.

Drums. So faint only a Hunter could hear them, coming from north through the water. The rapid beat meant a sacrifice was underway. The cabal of thirteen demoniacs would sacrifice an innocent and—if the blood pleased their unholy liege—they'd ask to curse an enemy with sickness or ill fortune or death. It rarely worked, as far as the Hunters could tell, but the demoniacs kept trying. They all deserved what was coming to them.

He stepped into the waters as quietly as he could. The cold mud washed into his high boots. It did not matter. All that mattered was destroying the shrine, and all those who worshiped at it.

Through a veil of sedges and bulrushes, the torches of the thirteen demoniacs illuminated the shrine. The statue stretched at least seven feet tall. The demoness had six arms—three on each side—and a belt of skulls as her only clothing. Her unmoving stone face may have been beautiful, were it not for the telltale tentacle beard of her mouth. On her head was a crown. This was the demoness Maeliik, the female aspect of Baa'oul prince of sloth and gluttony. So often their two aspects had no similarities; while Maeliik was a beautiful, black-hearted temptress, Baa'oul was an enormous hungry slug.

He repressed a shudder at the stone, lying in the midst of the marsh where none would find it. *None but me,* Pyoter thought. *None but a Hunter.*

The shapes of the demoniacs—in the flickering torchlight—eventually became distinguishable. Many he did not recognize—with Varister having five-thousand souls, that came as no surprise—but a coldness settled into his gut as the realized there were some he did. One was Mathise, a vestal of Seladora from a nearby convent. That in itself was enough for Pyoter to hate mankind forever, but it was another—Gaither Utheris—the bloody *magistrate* of Varister, in a purple cloak and a fine green tunic.

It is not just the lowly and demented that participate in this. The magistrate himself is a demoniac. He gave a second's thought to how Gaither's death would affect the town of Varister. Then he remembered it didn't matter how blue-blooded a person was; demoniacs deserved death. He reached down to pack on his first bolt.

In a small case of iron-and-adamant alloy lay Pyoter's most dangerous and effective weapon. Quietly he opened the case, and laid bare the weapon, biting his lip to steady himself. The bolt of white crystal—sparkling in the moonlight—would endanger no one if it weren't for the scintillating magic, ready to explode at the slightest disturbance. Bought at a hefty price, the Pontifex transported them from the impossibly-distant city of Zoar and into the hands of the Hunters.

Knowing a single slip could rend his body to the bone, Pyoter laid the bolt onto his crossbow. Though he'd demolished countless shrines in this fashion, it had always been done at great risk. *A risk worth taking,* he reminded himself as he watched the demoniacs dance around their grotesque shrine. Then he shot.

A half-second after the bolt flew, it struck. The latent magic energy within the white crystal burst at the impact. The demon queen's stone head hit the marsh-water next to Pyoter, splashing him and drenching his coat. When he looked up, water dripping from his wide-brimmed hat, the demon-shrine had turned to rubble, and its worshippers—once dancing and chanting—stumbled about, confused, severed from their infernal link. It was at this point, in the shock of their separation, that the Hunters acted.

Dropping the crossbow, he drew his dagger and ran toward the ruined shrine.

One by one, he put them to death by edict of the Pontifex. Long ago, in his greenhorn years of Hunting, Pyoter had difficulty carrying out his liege's demands. Over time it grew easier; over time and experience. When you had seen a cabal of demoniacs sacrificing an innocent, you never forgot it. They were beyond help, Pyoter told himself as he dispatched them one-by-one. The drums lay unattended; the victim—a slave, by the look of him—was long gone, a ritual-knife buried in his chest.

Hunting was grisly work. *I deal in death,* Pyoter realized. Murder—just or not—was his trade. By the time he'd gone round-circle, with twelve demoniacs dead or dying, he came to the magistrate's face.

The confusion had left the Gaither's brown eyes. The absent dullness had given way to the shallowness of fear. He turned to run, but Pyoter grabbed him by his collar and yanked him back. "Why?" Pyoter said, not knowing why the word had left his lips. He had never asked a demoniac anything before, only ended their lives without hesitation. But seeing Gaither's brown eyes, the noble face that led the people of Varister, and the costly purple tunic that marked his wealth and high position, he asked again. "Why? Why serve a demoness when you have everything?"

"I do not have everything," Gaither answered. "I do not have as much as others do. But I beg of you, my signore, do not kill me. I can give you gifts the padisha emperor would envy, if you only keep me alive."

"Keep you alive," Pyoter sneered. He kicked Gaither hard, and he staggered backward, splashing into the water. "You deserve to eat worms, Gaither. You deserve—" He stopped himself from saying more. He hurried toward him, entering the chill water, dagger in hand.

Gaither emerged from the water, half-swallowed in the muck, gasping for air. "Why kill me?" he screamed. "I have seen the error of my ways. You have shown me the light."

Pyoter grabbed him by the arm to prevent him from running. He forced the dagger against Gaither's neck, so hard it was a wonder he did not bleed. Still, Pyoter realized what he had to do. It was against protocol; against the express orders of the Pontifex and the Magisterium itself. But he would not put this foul life to waste. The demoniacs were sworn to silence under threat of their infernal lieges, but under the supervision of the Inquisitors, truth pours out of the vilest evildoer. "Yes, I will keep you alive," Pyoter went on, "but in time you will wish I had not."

CHAPTER FOUR:
INQUISITORS

Pyoter Matheris, Hunter

If the Hunters were the hounds of the Magisterium, the Inquisitors were the doctors; the prey, once caught in a Hunter's net, needed the truth extracted from them. And Pyoter couldn't help but smile as an Inquisitor in his long red robes took Gaither Utheris into the Red Chamber.

They bound him, hands and feet, by taut rope. Suspended in the air, the former Magistrate of Varister's pleas—"Let me down!" "I will do anything!" "Please, gods above save me!"—went unanswered.

"Tell us the truth," the head inquisitor said as two of his underlings readied their whips. "If you speak honestly, you will survive the ordeal. If you speak falsely, you will not. It is as simple as it sounds. And now, the first matter of business. What are the names of the other demoniacs in Varister?"

"There are none! As far as I kn—"

He had not finished speaking before the first whip cracked against him. The glass-covered thong opened a wound and tears streaked Gaither Utheris' cheeks.

Pyoter looked away and wondered if he could bear this. A knife to the heart, a quick kill for a dark deed, was something he'd grown accustomed to. But the Inquisitors had a shadowy reputation in the Magisterium and a far worse one in the wider world; and now, seeing their handiwork, Pyoter saw why.

"The truth!" the High Inquisitor shouted. "Who are the other demoniacs in Varister?"

"None!" Gaither whimpered.

Another whip cracked, another wound opened. "Wait!" Pyoter snapped. "Perhaps he is telling the truth. Perhaps..."

"A demoniac always lies at first," the High Inquisitor said.

"Surely you understand. I have extracted truth from the most egregious of villains. You hunt the Dark One's servants; and I pry the truth from their lying lips. Let us both respect each other, no?"

Pyoter bit his lip.

"Who are the other demoniacs in Varister? Speak truthfully," the High Inquisitor went on, "or you will get two lashes."

Tears trickled down Gaither's cheeks. "There are none in Varister!"

A glass-covered thong tore the skin from his bare leg. He shrieked.

"But I know of others!"

The other junior inquisitor was ready to whip him again.

"Wait!" the High Inquisitor snapped. "Fiorro, go fetch a bowl of salt."

The junior inquisitor on the left turned and left the chamber. At the word *salt*, Gaither began to weep.

"Tell me, Gaither, and tell me true. Who are these other wicked demoniacs you know of?"

"They are everywhere, Your Honor, in places high and low," Gaither choked through the tears. We stay within our cabals. But if you swear to me, that you will let me go, I will tell you one man's name... he is the leader of a cabal, a man of great importance."

The High Inquisitor laughed. "Of great importance to the Enemy. Very well, Gaither. Speak."

"Will you let me go?"

"Look where you are and look where I am," the High Inquisitor intoned. "You are in no place to bargain."

The other junior inquisitor, Fiorro, returned with a bowl of salt. Pyoter flinched. Gaither screamed.

"Tell me, demoniac, and tell me true," the High Inquisitor spoke, sounding patient and collected. "Else, you will be sorry. I have ways of keeping a man near death alive. If you lie, you will plead for the whips and salt; the Inquisition has much more inventive ways of torture."

"Will you let me go?" Gaither gasped.

"Fiorro."

When Fiorro rubbed the salt on the wound, Gaither gave a wild scream that made Pyoter fall back against the wall, breathless.

"I will tell you, I will tell you," Gaither moaned.

"And you will tell me true, or there will be more salt, and worse things." Pyoter could hear the High Inquisitor's smile.

"There are twenty cabals in Imperial City." Gaither's voice had the weak tone of a man who had given up. "The greatest meets at night throughout the city. The leader goes by Black Snake. He frequents a tavern… the New Moon in the Market District."

"Names," the High Inquisitor said again. "I want a name, or more salt."

Pyoter bit his lip.

"He never told me. He has dark blond hair. He has blue eyes and a scar—" The high-pitched gurgling scream erupted again, echoing across the walls and stealing Pyoter's breath. Fiorro had pressed more salt onto the wound.

"Oh, you demoniacs think yourselves so clever," the High Inquisitor laughed, "but I can see your lies before you speak them."

Pyoter grabbed the doorknob and stumbled into the corridor, gasping for air. He vomited onto the stone floor. He had seen more death and torture than he ever wanted to see again. But he had gained something, even if it was only a little. Another name, another lead, another demoniac to hunt. *In Imperial City, at the New Moon Tavern, by the name of Black Snake.*

CHAPTER FIVE:
FAITHLESS

Malyrria Tyrenas

Malyrria pranced around the stage of the New Moon Tavern. Today, she was Hypatia, the Irksome Nymph, and her fellow actor Hierkanto was Brecko the Lord of the Satyrs. Tomorrow, who knew what she would be? Perhaps they'd leave Imperial City and its noise behind, head north toward the dry Central Valley or perhaps south toward Nichaeus to entertain some soldiers for once.

"I said, Hypatia, where do you think you're going?" Hierkanto's fake golden beard failed to convince Malyrria, but a quick glance toward the crowd proved they were transfixed.

Malyrria struck a pose, hands on her hips, breasts out, smiling bright. In the distance, her boss and sometimes-actor Jacento made the rounds through the distracted crowd's coinpurses. "Why, I'm not doing anything, Brecko. Why are you so suspicious? Have I done anything wrong? I promised to love you forever. I've put all the satyrs and goatherds and goats behind me!" The crowd erupted into giggles. "There is only one goat beard and two goat-legs and one goat—" Their helper Niko clapped his cymbals. "—that I love."

The crowd burst into laughter. Malyrria pivoted to face Hierkanto. Beneath his bare chest, his fake goat member stood on end. The crowd's laughter built to a pinnacle.

They are so easily entertained.

Once the laughter began to die down, she cried out, "Excuse me, Brecko! You know I will be faithful and true… and I will be back soon!"

Malyrria exited the small stage and took a seat in the shadows while Niko clambered on. Their troupe had performed on bigger and better stages throughout the Empire, but competition in Imperial City was stiff. For now, they'd have to settle for a little tavern in the Market

District. The barkeep would pay them with hot food and cheap wine, but Jacento's sticky fingers would take an unannounced entry fee. It was how their troupe did business these days. There were too many actors, and too few stages. Perhaps their troupe would perform at the Odeon someday, but in the meantime they could enjoy the spoils.

Everyone in the New Moon Tavern watched Hierkanto and Niko perform, oblivious to Jacento's thievery. All except one, she noticed… a heavy-set man with sandy blond hair, gazing at Jacento as he did his deed and saying nothing. His blue eyes had a cold, dead look to them. Malyrria's neck-hairs stood on end and a chill passed over her. She hoped to the gods this man would not tell the City Watch. Their troupe would never perform again in Imperial City if he did; but slowly the blond man's eyes turned back to the stage, and if Jacento's pickpocketing bothered him at all he made no sign of it.

Eventually, Malyrria's attention turned back toward the stage. She had a part to play, a faithless nymph, a role she'd assumed hundreds of times for bigger audiences. As she once again assumed her role, she made a conscious effort not to watch him, to peer into those cold blue eyes.

By the time twilight came, Malyrria and her troupe had finished their performance of *The Pursuit of Hypatia,* It was one of the least sophisticated plays she knew of, fodder for dumb crowds and folk who had little knowledge outside their own lives. When Malyrria ran away from home to be an actress—leaving behind all the pomp and frills of the House of Tyrenas in Bregantium—she had no doubts her friends thought she was crazy. They did not understand her passion for the stage, her addiction to the fawning eyes and ceaseless praise of the crowds. But just a few steps outside the New Moon Tavern, in the gutter of the Market District, it was easy—after a quick glance of the crowd—why her girlhood friends thought her insane.

A cripple in a torn-up gray blanket hunched in an alley, his collection-dish empty. A gaggle of children—orphans, no doubt, having only each other—walked around, begging for coin to no avail. The poor were everywhere, and very much uncared-for in Imperial City and throughout the Empire. Malyrria had been the daughter of a wealthy family who had nothing to fear. She had been a Tyrenas, with slaves attending to her every whim. *But when you are born rich, you never realize what you have.* For a second, she wondered if she made a mistake.

Then a voice, in a familiar fawning tone, said: "What a wonderful job you've done! Tell me, are you as faithless as Hypatia?"

Malyrria smiled turned around to face the tavern door, but when the icy blue eyes of the blond spectator met hers, she gasped and fell back a step, her smile vanishing. She forced herself to smile again, recovering with grace. "Ah! You surprised me. I am sorry, signore. What is your name?"

"What is my name?" He smiled. "I should ask the same of you. Is it Hypatia?"

Malyrria almost said *yes*. "No," she laughed. "It is only the name of a role I play."

"And what is your true name?"

"You are rather forward, signore! I am afraid I cannot tell you. It would spoil the next show." Malyrria found herself creeping backward. The man had a little white scar across his cheek, and Malyrria wondered where he got it. He was big enough to be a legionary, but he did not have the muscle.

"Do you have a husband?" the man asked.

Gooseflesh spread over Malyrria's neck. Her intuition had been right. Behind those cold blue eyes was a person she should do all she could to avoid. "Ah, you are very forward, signore. I'm afraid I must go." She walked toward the entryway of the New Moon, and before she reached it the man's thick sweaty fist was around her arm.

"I know what you did," the man sneered. "I saw your little friend picking coins out of pockets. I'd answer my question, if I were you."

"What do you want from me?" she shrieked.

"The truth."

"I am unmarried," Malyrria breathed. "I have never been wed."

A yellow smile crept over the man's mouth, as yellow as his hair. Malyrria turned and ran. She wondered what this man wanted, who he was and what he was. She would lock her doors tonight, and stay close to Jacento. She could feel the man's gaze on her neck until she plunged headlong back into the safety of the New Moon.

CHAPTER SIX:
PASSAGE

Astarthe

Wherever Issachar had struck her, black-blue welts developed overnight. They racked her with pain at the slightest touch, and even when they did not touch her, the memory filled her eyes with tears. She had saved their lives, all three of them—hers, her brother's, and their Godling caretaker's—but Issachar told her never to use the *gleaming*, not even when her death was imminent. Because of the *gleaming*, they were alive today, and the Tiger Queen would let them leave.

With Issachar leading the way, they made their way through the streets of Saidoon. Stepped stone pyramids towered above gravel roads. Tigers—orange and black, or the sacred albino—lay down in the midst of the streets or walked through the reverently-parting crowd. Issachar said the tigers would never harm a Saidonian—their bonds were too strong—but they were not from Saidoon. Issachar said that Astarthe and her brother were from a far-away land to the north, that they were the rightful king and queen. But now they lived as outcasts, and who knows where they would live next? Sur, maybe, the Land of Elephants. Or perhaps they would beg for refuge in the Spice Cities. Either way, they would have no rest. They would never find a home. They had never spent more than a year in one place; Astarthe's only friend was her brother Anakh, and Issachar when he wasn't in one of his dark moods.

The markets of Saidoon were as noisy as ever. A man of Sur shouted at them in his jabbering accent—"Amulets! Lucky!"—and offered a fetish of an elephant, carved from ivory, clutched tight in his amber fingers. Beyond, half again as tall as the Sur-man and much larger than the folk of Saidoon, was a Sea Raider. Astarthe could tell by the dark shadows of his eyes, the earrings, the lip-rings, and the loose linen robe. Beyond, his many-sailed ship lay snug in the harbor, twice the size of the largest Saidonian barge or Fharese dhow. The Sea Raiders rarely visited Saidoon, though Astarthe heard they did not live far.

Issachar slowed to a stop and Astarthe stopped behind her. Anakh stopped a half second later and she clutched his hand.

The Sea Raider was talking with one of the Tiger Queen's women—important, Astarthe knew, because she had her hair braided with gold thread. Her long silk robe was blue, not purple like the queen, but it was still too expensive for anyone except the queen's women.

"What do you mean? The padisha is in danger!" she snapped, so angry she spat. "You raiders have no loyalty! I assure you, Her Highness will have no part in this scheme."

"There are enough riches in Taifun to double all your lady's holdings." The Sea Raider growled his reply. "There is enough wealth—"

"There will never be enough riches to take away her shame."

"Let me speak with her," the Sea Raider growled. If he meant it as a question, it sounded like a command.

"Her Highness has no use for faithless pirates," the queen's woman snarled in return.

"Is it because I am a man? There are women on my ship if you'd like to speak with them. I hear—"

She spat in his face, and his dark eyes bulged. "A curse on you and your family, forever!" she hissed. "May Senchin claw you to death and devour your heart. My denial of you has nothing to do with your sex, and everything to do with your request. Wicked fool of a man. Be gone from our harbor, or I will send the queen's spearmen after you."

The raider wrapped his giant brown hand round the hilt of his saber. A tiger snarled. Anakh looked back, and found a white tiger with blue eyes just feet away, ready to pounce. The raider jolted and backed away from it. The white tigers were the most revered of all.

"You have angered Senchin's child," the queen's woman

laughed. "Her Highness's city is filled with them. Get out, wicked fool, before they devour you! And if they do not, we will bind you and feed you to the Mother Flower. Run!"

The white tiger snarled again, and the raider broke into a sprint. Other tigers looked up from their slumber; a few followed him.

When the noblewoman's light brown eyes met Astarthe, they held no more warmth than they did while talking to the raider. "You. The Circle of Women saw what you did to the queen's mind. To this hour she denies it, says she had a genuine change of heart. I know better. You had best get out of here, if I were you. Little girls have been fed to the Mother Flower for less."

"Shut up!" Anakh snarled and lurched toward her. Issachar struck him across the face.

His painted eyes regarded the queen's woman. "We will be going momentarily."

Her glare built to a pinnacle. Then she whipped around and stormed off, disappearing into the crowd.

Issachar had a stormy look to his face. "Why has Atman cursed me with the care of two little fools? There is a reason I told you not to use your witchery, Astarthe, you spoiled little brat. And Anakh, your reckless anger will be the end of you in time, if you don't learn to control your emotions." His eyes narrowed. "Come with me, fools. You are lucky I have not given up on you yet."

Sometimes, Astarthe wished he would.

Anakh

He'd had just about enough of Issachar, and just about enough of Saidoon. The weather never changed; it was always boiling, and the only relief was the ocean breeze. They hadn't eaten a single scrap of meat since they came to this hellhole. There was only mango and coconut and jungle fruit, or if he was lucky, vegetable soup so spicy it burned his tongue. It was a wonder he hadn't run away by now, away from the Tiger Queen and her Circle of Women, away from Issachar the cross-dressing eunuch that beat his sister. His sister was the only reason he didn't run. Without Anakh, who knew what that fiend Issachar would do to her?

Barefoot on the gravel, he followed Issachar's flowing robe and thin womanlike neck. He touched his sister's hand, then held onto it. Whatever happened, he wouldn't let Issachar or the Tiger Queen nor the god Atman himself hurt her. She needed him just like he needed her. Through all Issachar's schemes and journeys, she was the only one he trusted. She was the only one he loved.

Loved.

Issachar said as soon as she came of age, as soon as she began changing from girl to woman, they'd be wed. When he argued, Issachar would overpower him and strike him, and Anakh was still too little to fight back. When he got big and strong like the warriors he'd seen, Issachar wouldn't be able to stand against him anymore. Anakh wouldn't have to listen to his tirades. Anakh wouldn't have to hear his insults or do what Issachar wanted him to do. It would be the beating of a lifetime when Anakh got big and strong. Then, he and his sister—wife or no—would live their lives as they wanted, and Issachar's thin, spindly fingers would no longer pull their strings like puppets.

Slowly, Issachar led them to the harbor. The many-sailed raider ship was their only possible destination. The only other was a dragon ship from Sur, and that land was too far away even for Issachar, though Anakh knew their "caretaker" would enjoy their misery. He glared at Issachar, waving and shouting for attention. The Sea Raider from before—twice as heavy as Issachar, and much braver, likely—stopped at the entrance ramp for the ship to regard him.

"What do you want, miss?"

Anakh burst into laughter. He liked this Sea Raider. He hoped he would journey with him. Maybe the Sea Raider would kill Issachar, and Anakh could join the crew, pledge himself to the bey, and live the adventurous life he'd always wanted... the adventurous life Issachar did his best to stop. Yes, he hoped this would work out.

If the Sea Raider's words unsettled him, Issachar forced himself not to show it. "We want passage on your ship. I can pay. I have silver and gold, and we will keep to ourselves. You have nothing to fear from us."

"Fear you?" the Sea Raider laughed. "I do not fear a cross-dresser and two children. That much, I assure you."

"Very well," Issachar said calmly. "I can offer you five gold pieces for passage. Where are you going?"

A yellow smile crossed the Sea Raider's dark, panther-like face. "We are meeting first at the Isle of Birds. Ayadd, bey, and his ships are meeting there. Then we sail for Taifun, and invade while the city lies undefended. If that is something you do not mind, you may feel free to join us."

Issachar turned his womanly face back at them, looking uncertain. If he refused, Anakh might kill him once and for all. Astarthe gasped for breath, her face white. Issachar regarded the Sea Raider once more. "We will go."

"Very well," the Sea Raider said. "You may call me Master Izeem."

Master, like a slave. Or maybe the Sea Raiders had different customs.

"On my ship, everyone calls Izeem master—man, woman, and child. You have no fear of slavery, here. Worse captains have sold passengers into bondage, but Izeem does not." His yellow smile widened, and then he turned to board the ship.

There were women among the Sea Raiders, with the same dark eye shadows as the men and long lush hair. A handful wore veils like married women did in Fharas, but many did not and moved about the ship as freely as the men. Some had scimitars tied to their belts. A good many were beautiful, Anakh realized, though he knew he had to be discreet. In the pirate cities where they came from, he'd heard of the punishment for a foreigner touching a free woman, and it would render him infertile forever. And if Anakh was infertile, there would be no more Anakhs and Astarthes left, no one with a claim to the Red Throne of Haroon.

CHAPTER SEVEN:
AN OMINOUS TASK

Tiverio Lucullus, Maestro of Foreign Affairs

After the Paladian, Mather Varis, left the Imperial Palace, things went back to their usual routine. The news came in as Tiverio Lucullus liked it: the legions on the Wall report no sign of barbarian incursion; more Fharese peasants trickled in from the southern border, which Emperor Severus now allowed alive; and throughout the cities of the Empire itself, there seemed to be no real trouble, no slave rebellions or blatant corruption.

It seemed all was well until a messenger arrived late one morning, bearing a scroll. The seal was the Hieronian eagle of the Pontifex, and the messenger had the telltale moustache of a Paladian.

"Your Undying Glory," the messenger said, "words from Pontifex, chosen of the gods."

Severus' lips pressed into a firm line. "Read."

He broke the seal and unraveled the scroll. "Your Undying Glory: Because you are sovereign of our Empire, I have decided to warn you first. The Inquisitors of the Magisterium have determined that at least twenty cabals of demon-worshipers operate in Imperial City. As shepherd of the people, I warn you that I have sent a member of the Revered Order of Hunters to discover the names and residences of these vile men and women, to be read for summary execution. If a man bears a letter granting him my permission to search or investigate, please advise your officials to comply. — An Eternal Blessing Upon You, the Pontifex."

Severus stood up and snarled. "That is outrageous! *Demon-worshipers*, in our city! Tell the Pontifex I shall help him in whatever way I can. I shall look forward to flaying the fiends alive." Though old and white-haired, Severus moved quickly, almost as quickly as the former emperor Claudian. "Tell the Pontifex I will allow his Hunter to search wherever he decides in Imperial City, without restriction."

"Thank you, lord emperor." The messenger bobbed his head and turned to leave.

Demon worshipers. Until the recent past, the Pontifex had asserted vehemently one thing: that there were only gods and god-haters, the Holy Beings and evil men. He had said demons were figments of a primitive mind, creatures designed to scare and frighten children, nothing more than superstition. Now the Pontifex had created an entire new order to hunt demon-worshipers, and preached regular sermons decrying those who worshiped the evil beings of darkness. It was anyone's guess if the Pontifex had always believed that demon-worshipers lived among the upstanding citizens, or if he had only recently admitted it. Still, Tiverio Lucullus wasn't sure what, or whom, to believe.

Emperor Severus still stood on his old legs. "We cannot let the public know. They will go into hysteria. It will confirm all the scary stories. They will believe every tall tale they hear in the taverns of Imperial City. I will comply fully, but we must root out this problem in the quiet."

"Of course," Lucullus answered. Besides the two Imperial Guards always at his side, he was alone. It would not leave his lips, but he would keep a watchful eye.

"There is something I wish you to do, Lucullus. Something I am not entirely comfortable with, but alas, it is necessary. This trouble in the Southern World… you are one of the only men I know who speaks the tongue of Fharas. I will send you as an emissary. I need to know all that is going on—"

No. Lucullus almost said it, but he had too much decency, too much respect for the shepherd of the people and his Undying Glory.

"—and I wish you to bring back a detailed report. That way I will know what needs to be done… if this is the perfect time to deal a death-blow to Fharas and her King of Kings. But you must go under the pretense of friendship."

"Of course…" The word was strained. Lucullus thought of

his wife, his two toddling sons, his daughter. *What will Vera do?* Perhaps he'd take his wife with him. But that would be cruel to her. Either way, she would not take the news well. "You do realize, Your Undying Glory, that the enemy Fharas fights may be worse than Fharas herself. It may be best not to—"

"Ah, Lucullus, you do not know what you speak of. The emperor Claudio destroyed the Fharese, stole Khazidea from them. Their destruction would be his heart's desire. And surely you would not argue with Claudio the Divine."

You are not Claudio, Lucullus thought, *nor even an Adamantus, only adopted in.* Still, he would argue no further with his Undying Glory. And he would have to depart within the week. Winter was near; the month of Anthanos was only a fortnight away. He would beat out the winter storms. He thought of Khazidea and its fertile plain, the Imperial road that followed the Khazan's infinite banks before stopping in the Desolation. Lucullus stared at Severus' wrinkled, ancient face, his shoulder-length white hair. He wondered if he would die at the hands of the Fharese tyrant-king. And he wondered, as he stared into Severus' blue-gray eyes, if His Undying Glory did not care.

By the end of the week, as he expected, he had already bidden farewell to Vera, embracing her as she wept inconsolably. At dawn he departed on an Imperial ship with sixty legionaries—a century, roughly—and left for a land he'd never been to nor wanted to go. Lucullus would have been happy if he stayed in the north his entire life and never saw the crocodiles of the Khazan River, nor laid eyes on the furthermost southern lands. He was maestro of foreign affairs, but as Imperial City disappeared behind him, he began trembling all over, and no prayers or words of encouragement from the soldiers could take away the thought that he sailed to his death.

CHAPTER EIGHT:
MERLING FOLK

Astarthe

Sometimes, when Astarthe looked into a person's eyes, the *gleaming* power within her would tell her something. When the Sea Raider captain, Izeem, spoke to Issachar, a cold dread had filled her. She could only tell he had not said all he knew. She could only tell enough from that little spark of *gleaming* that Izeem could not be trusted. Of course, anyone with a bit of knowledge about the Sea Raider folk knew they could not be trusted. Issachar certainly knew. Anakh seemed a bit overeager. But Astarthe would do her best to keep her distance from them.

They had been on the sea for three days. Astarthe had gone out onto the deck every once in a while, and never once seen any land. The constant rocking of the ship made her nauseous, but she would not complain. Still, she hated traveling the ocean. Astarthe could read, and she read all she could in the cities they stayed at. The South Sea was the graveyard of so many ships. So much water separated the land of the Tiger Queen and the mainland coast of Fharas.

So much water, so much danger, she thought throughout the course of that morning and felt tears well up. She would praise Issa, goddess of dance and love, when her feet were on the ground again. She reminded herself that the typhoon season was mostly over. She reminded herself that there were no Sea Raiders to overcome their ship and massacre them all, because she traveled with Sea Raiders and they did not harm their own. Still, the tears dripped down her cheeks, and in her weaker moments she trembled.

She clutched the railing as the ship rode the waves, bobbing up and down and splashing the deck. She felt someone's eyes on her, someone's attention fixed on her—a power of *gleaming* she could not suppress for Issachar's sake no matter how hard she tried—and then footsteps.

"Little girl." The woman's Fharese was strained, with a heavy accent. "Do not be afraid."

Astarthe turned and looked up. A Sea Raider woman, unveiled and unmarried, towered above her. She wiped away Astarthe's tears with her coarse fingers.

"Izeem means you no harm. He is a good man. He is not an oath-breaker. If he lied to you and broke his oath, he would throw himself to sea."

Instead of stopping her tears, the woman's words made them fall more thickly than before. She gasped and wept, clutching her leg like the mother she never knew. The Fharese padisha killed Mother and Father, Issachar said, on the vile northmen's orders. Issachar said he was both her mother and her father, but he was good at neither. He never reassured her like this woman did; he never ran a hand through Astarthe's hair like this woman did even now.

"Do not fear the sea, either, my little bird. The time of the sea's anger is passed. Mother Ocean is a good mother, and even when she claims the folk that belong on land, she gives them rest. Everything will be all right, little bird. Calm yourself. Calm, calm, calm. Hush…"

"What is your name?" Astarthe wept.

"Zaira, my little bird. Everything will be all right. Tonight I would sing you a song, but we will be on land before sunset. Then we will rest a while, and you will feel safe again until we set out for Taifun."

Land. This Zaira knew how to comfort her. To have her feet planted firm on the ground, even for a little while, would soothe her. To be on land with Zaira, even better. The tears fell again, this time from joy.

A thunderhead appeared in the distance, a quickly approaching wall of purple, and neither Zaira's words nor the temporary calmness of the sea could stop Astarthe from trembling all over and weeping. The Sea Raiders were calling out, sounding frantic.

If the sailors aren't worried, you should not be either. Issachar's words—spoken a year ago, when they took a ship from the mainland—now did the opposite. She crumpled, knees on the floor, tears dripping thick down her cheeks. *I am too young to die,* she pleaded with the goddess Issa.

A hand grabbed her shoulder, slender and feminine yet large, and Zaira's familiar musk swelled over her. "We will get you below deck. A little girl has no use in a storm."

In a creaking, dripping room, Zaira loomed over Astarthe, Anakh, and Issachar as the storm raged around them, winds howling and waves tossing the ship to towering heights before pulling it to breath-stealing lows. Of all the places to die, Astarthe would pick sea the last. "I am too young," she sobbed. "Issa protect us."

Through a glaze of fear, Issachar's eyes had the same scoffing derision. If Anakh was afraid, he didn't show a sign of it, like always.

"You are young, you say!" Zaira shouted above the creaking wood, the pelting rain and the ghostlike, shrieking wind. "So I shall tell you a tale old, so old it came before the Tiger Queen landed on the Verdant Land! When the womb of Mother Ocean birthed the fish and the sharks and the folk of Zubay…"

That is what the Sea Raiders call themselves, Astarthe remembered, and the ship took another dive. Water ripped across the ship's sides, and water poured in through the boards. Astarthe bit her lip to prevent herself from crying.

"South of the mainland, south of the Isle of Birds, beyond even the Verdant Land of plenty… there lies, hidden in darkness, the *Dark Continent*, where all evil has its beginnings, where the ever-present trouble of man is ever-eager to wreak its destruction. Molkoro, where the Taint lives."

The ship climbed another wave, but Astarthe forced herself to listen to the story.

"In the early years of Mother Ocean's birth, the land of Zubay had its golden years! The bey, Rasheem the Magnificent, had a palace built of gold, and reigned in a city with golden streets! There was no want of food! The ships brought in ivory from Sur and spices from the East and sun-bronzed wheat from the mainland! But Rasheem Bey, even having everything and lacking nothing, wanted the world!"

The ship plowed into water, but Astarthe forced herself to listen despite her trembling fingers.

"Rasheem the Magnificent, lord of all Zubay, raided every city in the lands of the ancients. But word reached Rasheem there was a land he had overlooked… Molkoro, the Dark Continent, did not call Rasheem its lord. And so, with all his ships, and all the fighting men of Zubay, he sailed to this insolent land. In the shallows he set anchor. And armed with machetes, he cut furiously through the undergrowth! *He was never seen again!*"

Astarthe gasped and the ship rocked precariously.

"All the fighting men of Zubay, all the great ships, disappeared into the darkness of the jungle! And that is where the story ends! To any lesser tale-teller, the Story of the Lost Fleet ends right there! But I have gone to the land of the Taint, and I have seen the Tainted City where the skeleton of Rasheem lies, buried amidst its accursed gold. The tribes who live in shadow still hunt their prey, the women and men who come from Mother Ocean! No game to them is better than men and women like you, like me! No feast is better than—"

"*Enough!*" Astarthe screamed, and try though she did, a spark of *gleaming* bled out through her words, chilling the room. Zaira fell back against the wet wooden wall; within seconds, the winds had died down and within minutes the storm had vanished completely.

Anakh

The next day, in the morning's light, Anakh climbed above-deck. There was no sight of the woman from before, neither in the room they stayed in nor on deck. In the distance, a rocky island stood out against the calm blue waters. Other raider ships had anchored off the coastline.

On Izeem's ship, whose name he still did not know, the sailors went about their duties calmly. Anakh could tell they had calmed down; they were relaxed, now, even joyful.

Izeem, at the head of the ship, was talking loudly to a Fharese slave: "It is not superstition. Have you ever seen a storm calm itself so quickly? There was a merling witch on our ship. The only reason we are not in the briny depths is that someone killed her."

"Merling folk!" The slave's incredulous snort sounded half-hearted.

Perhaps he had not been to sea long. Izeem's story seemed credible, as far as Anakh knew. Izeem knew what he talked about; he hadn't lied, and the storm had calmed itself with a strange speed. There *had* been a merling witch on the ship, and Anakh had a hunch as to who it was.

"Once we drop anchor, we will do a head count," Izeem grumbled. "We will see who it is, who we thought we could trust…"

Anakh hurried across the deck, feet pressing against groaning boards. "Master! Master Izeem!" Anakh never called anyone master, but it was easy to see why people used it with Izeem.

"Useless little boy. What could you possibly want?"

"I know who the merling witch is… it's Zaira!"

"Zaira!" Izeem laughed. "I'd keep your tongue in your mouth, boy, before it gets cut off. Zaira was next only to our first mate, a good woman and brave."

"Then where is she?" Anakh snapped, maybe harshly, but Izeem only smiled.

"Very well, child." Izeem's sparse yellow teeth had the look of a hungry jungle-cat. "If she is aboard and you disrespected a crew member, I will deal with you as seamen do… I'll toss you to the sharks. Or perhaps I'll act a mainlander for once… I'll burn you alive on the Isle of Birds, like the magi do."

Anakh only narrowed his eyes, feeling heat rise up inside of him. Fear was for girls and for half-girls like Issachar. Anger was what boys felt. He wished he had a sword, a scimitar like Izeem. Then he'd challenge him. But instead, he just took deep breaths and relaxed his shoulders. He wouldn't fight Izeem, not yet.

Izeem lined up all the crew. Astarthe grabbed Anakh's hand. Zaira was nowhere to be seen.

"There were once seventeen of you, including these useless landlubbers," Izeem snarled. "Now I count sixteen. I guess the little brat was right. Zaira is gone. The merling witches grow more and more cunning by the year. She was the last I'd suspect. Gods damn it all! So now I want a confession. Who put the witch to death, gave her back to her vile Mother Sea?"

Silence followed. Astarthe squeezed Anakh's hand tighter. He met his sister's eyes, and she had that look of guilt, the look she had when she disobeyed Issachar and expected punishment.

"Tell me!" Izeem snarled. "*The Sun Ray* is my ship, and you are all lucky to ride her. If one of you doesn't speak, I'll cast lots and lop off a hand! Do *not* test me!"

The silence continued. Astarthe squeezed even tighter, and Anakh knew his sister had done something; moreover, he had an idea of what. He'd felt her use her power last night, and somehow Zaira, the merling witch, had been driven off, not killed.

"I heard a splash!" one of the crewmates snapped. "Last night, right before the storm calmed. I think... I think, Master Izeem, that she left herself."

Izeem laughed. "Merling witches never leave by themselves. They sink ships and drown sailors. You know that, Abir, as well as anyone else." Izeem frowned. "But so it is. If no one will take their reward, I'll cast lots. One unlucky mate will lose his hand. And our useless passengers are not exempt, no, not exempt at all." Izeem's yellow smile returned. "Who will it be? Will it be you, Abir? Will it be you, Sadeem?"

"Enough!" Astarthe said. "Izeem, she *did* leave by herself. I saw it. I might have had something to do with it."

To their left, Issachar snapped his head toward Astarthe, his painted eyes wide with that furious look they got when he was beating her.

"I am sorry, Izeem. I convinced her not to wreck our ship. It was me. Don't punish anyone else for what I did."

"Punish you?" Izeem laughed. "Ah, I knew the truth would come out. But you won't be punished, sweetling. I wouldn't strike a little girl, though you had fresh bruises when I first met you."

Issachar looked back toward Izeem. The Godling's once-pale cheeks turned a shade of pink. "Izeem—" he started to say.

It's good to see him embarrassed this once. Anakh smiled.

"*Master* Izeem."

"Master Izeem… the girl, she did play a part in it. But she hasn't told you the truth. Not the whole truth. She spoke with Zaira and eventually the truth came out, that she was an—ehrm—merling witch. So then I killed her myself, and tossed her body off the—"

"She told you she was a merling witch," Izeem laughed. "The first time a merling witch has ever told the truth. Oh, you are unconvincing, man-woman. The merling witches never tell anyone who they are. They build trust and then betray their 'friends' when they're miles out to sea, like we are now. They call up a storm and sink ships, drag sailors down and feast on their bodies in the depths of the water…"

Astarthe's hands were slick with sweat. Anakh didn't know if she was afraid of Izeem or Issachar.

"They have no friends, not even other merling folk. They have no love for anyone or anything but the water. If you meant to lie, man-woman, you did it terribly." Izeem turned his gaze to Astarthe. "You, little girl, if you defeated the merling witch by yourself, you are more needed on this ship than anyone else."

"I don't want to." Anakh's poor sister was trembling. "I don't want to," she repeated. "My place is on the land. I don't like the ocean. You said you would take me to the mainland. Zaira said she knew you.

She said you weren't an oath-breaker. She said the sea raiders don't break oaths."

Izeem howled with laughter. "There is no oath too precious for me to break, little girl. There is no vow too sacred to spurn. The mainlanders call us faithless and of all the things they say, that is the most true. *There is no friend I'd not betray*—so said Rasheem the Magnificent, the Sun Lord, the richest and greatest bey in history."

"Before he disappeared into the Dark Continent and lost his life to the Taint," Astarthe said, repeating the merling witch's story.

The amusement vanished from Izeem's face. His dark face lost half its color. "Where did you hear of such things? A little sweetling like you should not speak of such stuff. Where did you hear those stories? Does the Tiger Queen have a library no one knows of?"

"We have been many places!" Anakh snapped.

"Places of great learning," Issachar said, "and these two toddling children know more of the wider world than you likely ever will."

Izeem's hand went to the hilt of his scimitar.

"That said, they did not learn anything of Rasheem the Magnificent from books, and neither does the Tiger Queen have a library. The Sea Raiders are not any concern of the learned."

Izeem's dark-shadowed eyes bulged larger than Anakh had ever seen them.

"Zaira, the merling witch, told us all we know about him."

"The merling witch told you." Izeem laughed. His fingers shook as they gripped the scimitar hilt. "A friend of merling witches is no friend of mine. Ah, little girl. Perhaps I will keep you on the ship. But your little brother is useless to me. He will fetch a good price in the slave markets."

Anakh jerked forward, bristling, an insult on the tip of his tongue, but Issachar struck him on the shoulder and for once he listened.

"As for you, man-woman," Izeem snickered. "It would have been better if you picked one gender. The men of Zubay prefer their women to be women, and their men to be men. You'd have lived a few years in the sugarcane fields, maybe, like this spoiled little brat. We'll likely toss you to the sharks before we reach Taifun."

"*No!*" poor Astarthe screamed. "You won't take my brother and my mother and my father away!" The dank air chilled, and her voice had the sound of power. "You will not sell Issachar or my brother into slavery!"

Izeem staggered back, gasping for breath and touching his black hair. "Ah…" When he looked up again, his eyes were wide with wonder. "The little girl is a sorceress. The little girl… She tried to compel me, but my mind is too slippery for her. Toss her overboard, Abir! She's too dangerous. She'll be food for the merling witch, or worse!"

"No!" Astarthe screamed. "No!"

"Stop this at once!" Issachar screamed.

"*Gods damn you!*" Anakh rushed him; he had no sword or dagger but he'd tear off Izeem's skin with his fingernails if that's what it took. "If you lay a hand on my sister, *I swear by the Sun God himself—*"

He leapt for Izeem, ready to strangle him and rip his limbs off, but the giant pirate already had his scimitar drawn, and struck Anakh hard in the head with the pommel. Tears of pain filled his eyes as he hit the deck. He scrambled to his feet a second later to charge him again. Instead, he witnessed a Sea Raider mongrel lifting his sister above his beastly turbaned head. His sister—the only one he loved, the woman he was meant to marry, his only friend—stared at him with wide panicked eyes. As the ship drove through choppier and choppier waves, and a mountainous island appeared, jutting out of the sea, Anakh ran for her with all he had in him. He tripped over a leg— Izeem's—and hit the deck as that beastly Sea Raider tossed the only person he loved overboard. He had barely heard a splash when thunder clapped in the distance, and beyond the mountainous island, giant purple clouds rolled in like an army of chariots: a storm so fearsome it could split the Isle of Birds in half.

CHAPTER NINE:
THE FEAST OF SPIRITS

Malyrria Tyrenas

Before she and her troupe started work at the New Moon Tavern, Malyrria had loved the Feast of Spirits and all it stood for. She looked forward to all the tales of Red Satyrs massacring villages, of hungry revenants haunting abandoned temples, or, even more chilling, monasteries filled with evil monks. Now, the tales they told only made things worse, only made her ignored pleas to leave Imperial City more desperate. Jacento wouldn't hear of any of it; the New Moon was the first tavern to actually pay them as well as serve them food, even though Malyrria had become wary of the audience's faces, wondering why a tavern in the famously-competitive Market District had taken such an interest in their troupe—a group of five rascals that Fort Martello, a small town in the hot dry hell of the Central Valley, had shooed away.

Jacento only had eyes for silver and gold, and Hierkanto only had eyes for Jacento. Niko lusted for Malyrria and Nabia loved Malyrria like a sister, but neither enough to stand up for her.

Malyrria was on stage in her costume: a plain woolen gown, torn up from use, and a horn-of-plenty in her hands. She was Terrena, Queen of the Harvest. Nabia—standing across from her on the stage and dressed in black rags—represented Hunger.

"Ah, Terrena / Ancient foe / A woe upon you / Woe on woe!" Nabia could sing better than anyone Malyrria knew, good enough perhaps to leave the troupe altogether and do better for herself; that was why she played Hunger, the only singing part. Jacento had lightened her copper Khazidean skin to make her look sickly, darkened the shadows under her eyes, and instructed her to tremble; but even then she was the Nabia she'd known, the beautiful southron girl that men wanted and women envied.

Malyrria tried to mask her fear. "In autumn time, we draw the line. The line is drawn, the battle line. Will they hunger? Will they starve? The people of the mortal realm—"

"Stop!" The giant blond man rose up from the crowd—the man Malyrria tried to avoid. "I have a request. It is the Feast of Spirits—"

Her inner aristocrat forced its way out of the frightened shell. "How dare you! Were you raised in a barn? There is a show going on, and—"

"It is the Feast of Spirits, and you are all so talented. It is autumn, true, and the grain freights arrive each day."

At the sight of his dead, ice-blue eyes, the dignified Tyrenas within her shriveled, and she was the frightened Malyrria again.

"But it is, more truthfully, the Feast of Spirits. Tell me. Your repertoire seems endless. Do you know my favorite Feast of Spirits play? It is called *Last Rites for a Vagabond*."

Malyrria said "No!" and Nabia said "Yes!"

The blond man's smile widened. "Who shall I believe?"

"I do not know it," Malyrria repeated. "And do you know, good man, how rude it is to stop a play?"

Behind, near the door to the tavern, Jacento was glaring at her. "If they want to see *Last Rites for a Vagabond* then they shall see it."

"I do not know it," Malyrria repeated. It was a lie. "Someone else will have to do it. Hierkanto…" She turned and left the stage. When she finally vanished from the crowd's sight, she was trembling all over. In the darkness of the room, she felt safe from those blue eyes. But the man knew she was afraid of him, and it only made him bolder. She did not know what he wanted, but she did not want to know.

Behind stage, Hierkanto's blue eyes had a seething look. Perhaps already having heard the command, he had the black hooded cloak of Death—the part that Malyrria usually played—and skeleton gloves.

"You've really ruined things tonight," he growled as he draped the black cloak over his head.

Malyrria sank to the floor and knit her fingers together. She could flee north by herself, leave the troupe, head down the Path of Tidus all by herself. But it was near dark, and she wouldn't be out of Imperial City before night fell. At night, the streets of Imperial City became a wild no-man's land, and a girl walking by herself had as good as killed herself. She prayed to Lunas, god of actors and acrobats and all virtuous thieves that steal from the greedy: *Protect me. Give me alert eyes and a guileful tongue, sticky fingers and the moon's own luck.*

On the stage, in the flickering light, the play was beginning. Behind the stage, Niko pounded a drum. Hierkanto—dressed as Death—knocked air, pretending it was a door. "Eloesa, Eloesa, murderess, thief. It is time for you to leave this world for Heaven's judgment seat. Long have you lived, undeservedly; and now is come your day to die."

At the words, Malyrria buried her head in her hands and struggled to breathe. *Lunas, you let me live the life I wanted; you let me travel the world on a stage. Please, God of Actors and Acrobats and Virtuous Thieves, give us all the moon's own luck. Let your wife Selune cloak us in her starry cloak, safe from the poison arrows of the dark-hearted.*

"No! No! It is not my time! No! No!" Nabia—or Eloesa—shrieked, sounding genuinely afraid, but that only made Malyrria feel worse. "Another month! Another year! Please, Death, I have so much life left! You cannot do this to me! You cannot—"

"There is nothing you can offer me," said Hierkanto, in the cool, detached voice of Death itself. "Your time is come to be repaid as you have done in this mortal realm. As you have done, it will be done to you."

"I can offer you something!" Nabia shrieked; she had become Eloesa. She was so talented. But Malyrria stood up to walk away, not wanting to hear the rest of this demented play. "I can offer you something. The life of someone else. A sacrifice, so that I might live forever."

In the right circumstances, Malyrria did not mind the

demented playwright's imagination. But in this day, and in this hour, she could not bear it. She walked through the dark space filled with costumes and props, and took a side door outside, into an alley. The air had a slight chill that promised winter. It was The Feast of Spirits and she had to guard herself. She had to leave, but she could not.

It was late, and the barkeep served them a meager dinner. "Fresh bread," the cross-eyed, pudgy man told them, "made from good Khazidean wheat. Mother Khazan gave a nice flood, or so I hear."

Then, one by one, he poured wine into five lead wineglasses.

"For your great performance today, five glasses of sweet northern white. The Getans can't do much, but they know how to make wine." The barkeep gave them a lopsided grin, then turned and vanished into the candlelit dimness.

"Not as good as last night's," Jacento grumbled. He took a small bread loaf and broke it in half. "Last night, there was at least meat."

"Fish," Hierkanto corrected him playfully.

Down the table, Nabia chatted with Niko, looking like she didn't have a care in the world. Malyrria wondered if she'd been overreacting. How could she not be?

In truth, what is there to fear? What reason do I have to think I'm in danger? There isn't any substance to how I feel. Malyrria, for the first time in days, relaxed her shoulders and took a piece of bread. As Hierkanto and Jacento laughed, reminiscing of the good days long-passed, Malyrria joined in.

"Ah, Brilium you say?" she laughed. "I don't think it was all that bad, Hierkanto! And Jacento, I remember you telling me how much you liked the ale. I rather liked it. I mean, it's no Bregantium, but—"

"Bregantium," Hierkanto snorted. "Down here, they think *that's* a small town. Well, I'd like to see what these city-folk would think if they went that far north. Brilium has one thing going for it, sweet

Malyrria, and that's logging. Other than that, there is nothing." He grabbed his wineglass and guzzled the rest of it down. He laughed again and nearly choked.

"Slow down." Jacento smiled and took a deep sip of his own. His dark brown eyes met Malyrria's. "You haven't touched your wine, friend."

"Ah, yes. I suppose you're right." Malyrria grabbed her glass and took a deep gulp. It was nearly sweet as honey, a nice change from the harsh reds they'd been served the past few nights. "Ah, see? We Getans *can* do something right. We're better winemakers than the southerners."

"You are from Gad, but you are not a Getan." Hierkanto gave her one of those slimy, flirtatious smiles he used on anyone he was trying to charm, but he had no real love for Malyrria. "Your hair is a lovely brown, and you bathe near every day. You know a little of culture, and you've read at least one treatise on Thenoan Philosophy. You are from Gad, but you are not a Getan."

Malyrria smiled. "And you are an Eloesian to the core, Hierkanto. Looking down on anyone with a head of gold hair."

"There are gold-haired Eloesians, my sweet. It is not gold hair I look down on." Hierkanto's slimy smile grew slimier, slimy enough for Malyrria's body to respond to it. But he had no love for Malyrria, or Nabia for that matter. "Golden hair is not the issue. A lack of intellect is the issue." Hierkanto's eyes shut, and seconds later they had not opened.

Malyrria looked down the table and saw all the troupe members had fallen asleep in their chairs. She herself could feel exhaustion settling in. The barkeep had put something in their wine.

Out of the shadows, the blond-haired man from before emerged, now dressed all in black. In his right hand, he clutched a thin steel dagger. Behind him, more men and women appeared also wearing black—the patrons of the inn, now showing the wolves behind the lamb's clothing. Malyrria shrieked and choked on her wine.

"On the Feast of Spirits," the blond-haired man said, his

sharkish smile widening, "the unseen worlds converge on the worlds of the material. I shall not tell you my name, Malyrria, for none of us know each other's names. They call me Black Snake, and together we honor Log'ain the Betrayer. With your innocent blood we will embolden him, and in his power he will strike the Pontifex dead."

"You are mad!" Malyrria screamed. "You have gone mad!" She turned to run but the innkeeper's fat hand caught her. Holding her fast, they bound her wrists with rope. She prayed to Lunas, but it was only a resigned whimper, "Grant me the moon's own luck!"

The blond man, Black Snake, gave a long, deep, belly-laugh. "To the World Beneath we will go… a world beneath the simple folk of Imperial City, where the Lords-and-Ladies-To-Be lay plans and revel!"

"You are mad!" Malyrria screamed. "You are mad!"

At her words Black Snake's belly-laugh grew louder and deeper. A black-gloved hand thrust a cloth over her mouth; it smelled of death. In an instant, all was black.

~

When she awoke, she was tied to a chair in the midst of a stone circle. Around her, the flickering torchlight painted the narrow stone tunnel orange. *A sewer canal*, she realized, *or what used to be one.*

Looming above her, holding the same ritual knife, was a man who could only be Black Snake—the same heavy build and the same fat fingers, his face covered in a wolf-skin mask. Behind him were others, at least a hundred in clear view, some wearing pig-skin or wolf-skin masks and others wearing long black hoods.

"The Great Lord cometh," Black Snake bellowed. "Now his Name is only a whisper, but soon it shall be shouted from the highest mountain and the lowest dale. The Great Lord cometh, and his hour of ascension draws nigh."

"The Great Lord cometh!" the crowd chanted. "And his hour of ascension draws nigh!"

"You are mad!" Malyrria screamed. They had lost their minds. Tears formed in her eyes. She bucked and struggled, trying to the break the rope, but she might as well have tried to bend iron.

"It is time for the Great Unmasking!" Black Snake shouted. "Let the victim see those that shall be lords and ladies in the world to come! Let her look upon her future masters; who in her coming life shall hold all power."

One by one, the masks came off. Hiding behind a pigskin mask was a pallid woman with cold blue eyes, her blonde hair coiffed and braided, a pearl necklace hanging round her chest. Malyrria knew nothing of her except her obvious high position; she wondered how in Varda a woman of such privilege and dignity could believe in this insanity, even take part in it. Other masks came off; some with jewelry and some without, some dignified and aristocratic and some dirty and unshaven. One man, a hulk, towering above all the others, Malyrria recognized after she thought about it: the captain of the City Watch. She grew cold.

"Lord Log'ain," Black Snake bellowed, "consecrate this innocent life; from the power of her blood send your shadowy hand across the sea. With the vigor of her youth I curse the Pontifex with a horrid disease; let him die in horrid pain, and let him die alone!"

"Wait!" Malyrria screamed. "Wait! Your lord, Log'ain, will surely be given more power if he sacrifices more than one. I am not innocent. There is a woman, Nabia, who has never known love—and her sacrifice would please him more! And there are three others, too!" Perhaps she was wicked but she had a life to live. She couldn't afford to care.

Black Snake's smile doubled in size. "Ah! You impress me, actress. The Betrayer surely smiles within his infernal House. You have won us over! So many dare not forsake their friends. So many dare not forsake their gods. But you impress me, Malyrria. Will you pledge yourself to the Great Lord?"

"Yes!" Malyrria screamed. "Yes! Gods be damned! The Great Lord cometh, and I am his thrall!"

CHAPTER TEN:
SUN AND MOON

Anakh

They had barely reached the other Sea Raider ships when the storm arrived, churning the waves to immense size. Spears of lightning lit up the sky and the rain pelted with ever-increasing speed. Though Izeem was running around shouting, and men were dropping anchors, and panic had overtaken everyone, all Anakh could think about was Astarthe and how Izeem had thrown her overboard, and how—even though the great purple sky threatened death—all he wanted to do was flay Izeem alive, kill him like he killed Astarthe and make it a thousand times as painful. But his hands and feet were bound, now, and he couldn't walk, let alone attack the horrid Sea Raider who had killed his sister.

Birds swarmed throughout the giant mountainous island before them, but they were retreating in the face of the coming storm. The waves, even in the shallows surrounding the rocky beach, had grown near as large as they were last night, before Astarthe drove away the merling witch and saved the ungrateful raiders.

In an instant, the waves had grown just as large, then larger. The giant waves tossed the ship around like a toy in Anakh's bathing-pool. And somehow, the waves were dragging them further back, out to sea. With each pounding of the waves, Anakh slipped across the deck. As the purple clouds swept in, covering the sky, the spears of lightning grew ever closer and closer. The wood of the ship groaned, and then—as it slammed down from a high wave—a loud *crack!* echoed across the roiling seas, and the ship began to sink, even as some strange force pulled it, and the entire sea raider fleet out to sea.

Anakh's bladder emptied as the ship made its slow descent.

Eventually he realized, even as the ship retreated further and further out to sea, a whirlpool was forming, drawing in other ships as well. *The merling witch,* he thought, and no sooner did it dawn on him than she began to rise out of the sea. No longer was she Zaira, the raven-haired Sea Raider woman. Now, as her leaf-green webbed hands controlled the roiling waters, her green hair looked like seaweed.

"*Astarthe!*" Issachar screamed, and Anakh saw her too, a tiny form clinging to the merling witch's giant neck, a big smile on her pretty face.

For a moment Anakh could barely control himself. He ran to the railing of the ship, and Issachar followed just a second behind. When Anakh looked back at him, Izeem was running right behind, sword drawn.

"The merling folk may eat us!" he screamed. "But first I'll have both your heads!"

Anakh pushed Issachar over the railing, and he fell flailing into the water. Then he leapt over himself as Izeem's scimitar whistled through the air.

When they hit the water, the merling witch drew them both away from the giant eddy, even as the pirate fleet descended further and further toward the hole in the sea. She guided them all the way to where she treaded water, where his sister was, the sister that he loved.

"Faithless pirates, you get what you deserve!" the merling witch called out in a many-stranded voice that echoed over the water. Her yellow eyes bulged as she stared at the giant eddy. "And you two, the boy and the Godling, I shall deign to save. You I respect, and so too does the merling queen. I shall leave you on the Isle of Birds."

"That is all we want of you!" Issachar gasped.

The water kept Anakh afloat without any effort; he did not need to tread or swim. He breathed deep, but his muscles were tense, and he would not have any relief until both feet were on the ground. He knew full-well that time was coming soon.

The merling witch clenched her webbed hands into fists, and

the swirling eddy collapsed in on itself, closing over the fleet of pirate ships. The ensuing wave rippled across the sea and passed over Anakh without incident. Then she called up a current and sent all three of them—Anakh, Astarthe, and Issachar—straight toward the rocky shore.

Astarthe

Lying in the pebbles as the sea-foam washed over her, she felt her brother's hands where her breasts would one day bud. In all her eleven years of life she had never been apart from her brother Anakh. The hour without him had made him realize what she had. She loved him, she realized; and what Issachar had pressured her into doing no longer seemed so wicked. She remembered Issachar's words, how they were the last Anakh and Astarthe left, how the line of brother-kings and sister-queens had sat on the Red Throne for a millennium before the Destroyer sent them away. Anakh and Astarthe were destined to be one: king and queen, brother and sister, man and wife. The time was upon her. Her brother's eyes had a glazed, bestial look she'd never seen before, a look that frightened her, and for a second she hesitated, thinking of running away. But Anakh, and the part of him that made him a man had grown large, and it was too late to flee now. She bit her lip, afraid but knowing what she had to do. She prayed to Issa to give her strength.

"In the name of Atman the Progenitor, from whom comes all grain and green things of the Valley of Khazan," Issachar shouted, "and in the name of Issa the Fertile, whose tears of love flood the life-giving River of Khazan, and water the seeds… join these two who are your vicars, your living vessels in the mortal realm. Bless them as they become one, as you became one. Atman, Anakh; Issa, Astarthe."

When her brother finally entered her, it hurt her more than she expected; she had heard it was the childbirth that filled a woman with pain, and it was love that filled her with pleasure. Instead, she bit her lip so as not to cry out. But they were one; brother sister, king and queen.

"In the name of Lord Sun and Lady Moon, by the authority of the Progenitor Atman in whose service I am sworn, I pronounce you man and wife!" Issachar's voice sounded too loud to Astarthe, though only birds lived on this desolate isle. "Bless them, Atman, Lord Sun, and give them back the throne that rightfully belongs to them, the Red Throne of Haroon."

It isn't right, Astarthe thought. *A brother should not wed his sister.* It seemed wrong, it seemed so terribly wrong. But as Anakh—Atman—finished his deed, she could not help but feel it was right.

CHAPTER ELEVEN:
THE GATHERING STORM

Months Later…

Tiverio Lucullus, Maestro of Foreign Affairs

The stone walls of Fort Tidus appeared, and beyond lay the Desolation, what locals called "the place of poisoned earth." The journey had been as miserable as Lucullus expected, though he and his century had all the food and water he could ask for. The Khazan floods had been good this year, producing a surplus of grain. But the people—as he should have expected—were foreign to him: respectful, for the most part, and hard-working, but foreign. Their gods had the heads of animals and their priests—in some cases—wore the garb of women. Most repellant of all to Lucullus was the custom of heavenly prostitution, the girls ordained to serve the goddess of fertility Issa in her grand temples, taking on worshipers in her lustful embrace.

Now, in sight of Fort Tidus, the century of sixty legionaries did little to assuage the lump growing in his throat. Beyond the giant stone building, a bulwark against the southrons, lay the waste. The hardpan soil, the tragic product of many years of warfare, stretched into the indeterminate distance. It was late morning, but Lucullus was a government official and he had the final say.

"We will stay the night here," Lucullus ordered.

The centurion—an Anthanian named Valentus—gave a brusque nod. "Your Honor," he said. "I will see to it that the animals and your personal belongings are stored properly."

Lucullus smiled. He could not remember Valentus smiling, not once throughout the whole journey. But if Lucullus commanded Valentus to laugh, he would; he was that dutiful.

~

In the darkness of the fort, the commander of the Second Harak Legion sat down on a wicker chair in the light of the candle. His face was wrinkled and ashen, his lips colorless and thin. He had the look of a man who had given up; and so did the other legionaries.

"Finally, Severus has sent someone, that snake," the legate growled—Alesso, if Lucullus remembered right. "As soon as we stop petitioning him, he sends an unexpected guest."

In Lucullus's household, no one disrespected the emperor in word or deed, no matter how much they disliked him. But neither could he disrespect this honorable legate who had seen more blood and warfare than Lucullus likely ever would. "Has the emperor done something to insult me?"

"The perfect storm is brewing in the south," Alesso growled. "It is not an Imperial concern for now, but it will be: in a year, maybe, or in a decade. The padisha emperor lives in fear, never staying in one city more than a week. His subjects sever ties with him, fearing the Dark Horde."

"The Dark Horde?" Lucullus gulped.

"Severus told Mather Varis he would not help our ancient enemy. I say, we do not need to worry about them anymore." Alesso stood up. His silver eyebrows furrowed, and his blue eyes blazed, filled perhaps with a reignited fire. "I dare not say 'help them,' for that would brand me traitor. But if the padisha emperor is unseated, and the Four-Pointed Star never flies on any flagpost again, then what will take its place is much worse. The Dark Horde has poured out of the desert and they hold nothing sacred and hate everything that brings mankind joy."

"How do you know this?" Lucullus said, forcing himself to keep calm.

The fire left Alesso's eyes. His lips pursed into a thin line. "We have enough food for all of you. We have beer for all, too. Wine is not a Khazidean thing, friend. When you live in the Land of Issa, you must live like the southrons do." A weary smile touched his lips.

"As we have been living, then." Lucullus returned a smile, just as weary. "It takes getting used to, but twenty days down the Imperial Road through Khazidea, and I love barley beer as much as the natives."

"The Land of Issa has a way of doing that to you." Alesso's smile grew but remained weak. "Eventually you like the heat and you never want to leave sight of the Khazan. It is too bad I live here."

Though Fort Tidus, like most things in the province, was in view of the life-giving river, Lucullus would guess the Khazan took on a more ominous appearance as it wound its way through the hardpan, the "land of poisoned earth."

Over bread and barley beer, the centurions and the off-duty legionaries bonded, shouting and laughing uproariously as their leaders—Lucullus and Alesso—sat in the corner, drinking slowly and discussing more serious topics.

"I would go back if I were you," Alesso said at one point in the night, perhaps finally speaking from his heart. "The Southern World is at war. The Fharese army is weakened from the wars against the nomads but they are still strong enough to destroy you."

"I will offer him my help." Lucullus took a sip of his barley beer, the drink he had strangely come to love. "It sounds like he needs help."

"And will you help him?"

"I do not know." Lucullus frowned. "Emperor Severus says he wants me to gather information for the purposes of destroying the padisha's empire once and for all."

"Then you will hurt him."

"I do not know," Lucullus said. "If I were not a man of unswerving patriotism, dear Alesso, I would heed your advice. I'd wait a while, return, and tell him what you told me. But I have too much honor, Alesso."

"A good thing for a public servant. But be careful, Lucullus," Alesso pleaded. "Do not trust anyone and take nothing for granted. Do not even trust the emperor."

"I find it easy not to," Lucullus muttered, "though I am ashamed to admit it. I will be untrusting. It is something you learn as a member of the Imperial household."

"There are ghosts in the Desolation, tortured spirits of warriors and innocents. But even though they can suck all the blood from your veins, I'd fear them less than the storm in the South. Be careful, my dear Lucullus. Promise me."

"I promise I will be careful. I promise I will trust no one. I promise—"

"Hush." Alesso smiled. "Enjoy these hours while you still have no cares. The Khazidees have a saying I am fond of: there is no trouble, there is no war, there is no strife to a drinker of barley beer."

In response, Lucullus took a deep sip, and relaxed all his muscles. There would be stress enough for him in the coming days and weeks.

~

In the Desolation, a manmade desert of stinging salt, choking dust, and cracked earth, Lucullus made his way southward. There was no Imperial Road beyond Fort Tidus, though the way was clear: follow the river south until it bends east; then, beyond the land of the Rock Forts, lay the Southern World, a world in chaos.

In the whirling gusts of salt, sand, and dust, Lucullus thought he saw women's faces and the shrieks of the dead—the *mara* and *lilitu* the Khazidees spoke of—but it was of no concern to him. They kept south, south into a land at war. South into the gathering storm.

CHAPTER TWELVE:
THE SHADOW

Thelimer Utheris, Priest of Hieronus and All the Gods, Pontifex

From his vantage point at the highest level of the Magisterium, a high balcony that overlooked the City of the Gods and beyond it, the choppy waters of the Imperial Sea, the Pontifex removed his miter and set it to the side of his chair. He laid his golden rod lengthwise across his lap. It was time for the daily commune with the Lord of Order, Justice, and Just War. The unconquered god Hieronus was displeased, Thelimer knew, with what went on. The human kingdoms and principalities fought amongst themselves, men and women strove to gain wealth, and the people grew lax in their state of luxury, all while the Growing Dark slowly but steadily increased its hold on the material realm.

His proclamations that demons were at work, and most frightfully of all, that humans sacrificed to them to gain favors, had not been done lightly. Hieronus himself had commanded Thelimer Utheris, and all the protestations of the high priests would not cause Thelimer to disobey his god.

Hieronus, he said and shut his eyes, *speak to m—*

The air chilled, and he opened his eyes. He glanced around, seeing no one and nothing. But when he fixed his eyes outside, a black speck appeared in his vision, and it was growing in size. He stood up and turned to run, but before he even made a step the shadow was there—sometimes human, sometimes formless—and before he had taken another breath it struck him full on. Blackness consumed his vision; his body went chill and numb. His muscles turned to jelly, and he half-realized his knees had hit the floor. As he fell, he thought some affliction was tearing through his body—boils and sores spreading over his skin like gooseflesh—and then he fell into a sudden and evil sleep.

CHAPTER THIRTEEN: ILL OMEN

Claudian Adamantus the God, Monk Militant

Claudian shot up out of his stone bed in Cloud Temple Monastery. His loose monk's habit was wet, and he himself was covered in cold sweat. In his mind he felt Hieronus' words: *Trouble in the lowlands*, and just as clearly, *Do not leave the temple.* He told himself to listen. Eighty-one years of life had taught him to listen to the Lord of Justice and Just War.

~

In the morning, Claudian descended to the first floor of Cloud Temple. The initiates had scurried out of their beds before dawn and eaten their boiled roots. The giant pillars—etched with montane reliefs along their extent—gave a feeling of space to the already-giant antechamber. No fire warmed them, even here in the high mountain valley at the threshold of winter. The stone floor chilled Claudian's bare feet even further. But in the Order of St. Traber, a monk had no clothing but his habit, no friend except Hieronus and no weapons besides his body.

Claudian headed outdoors. In the dim early-morning light, he could make out a horseman approaching. *Eighty-one years old, and I can still see like a hawk.* There was a saying with more than a grain of truth: "A monk does not age; he only dies." Claudian's teacher had lived to one-hundred and one, still perfectly sane and able to run many miles. But eventually his death-day came. Eventually Claudian's death-day would come. But that was not his concern.

The cold mountain air hit him like a wall, and he strained to breathe. The messenger had something urgent to say—that much was clear, since the snow would come any day now, making the roads impassable—and Claudian would hear him out. But even then he reminded himself of the god's words in a half remembered dream: *Trouble in the lowlands. Do not leave the temple.*

At a gallop the horseman tore down the road. He shouted hoarsely, "I come from the Magisterium! His Honor the Pontifex has a message for Brother Claudian Adamantus, Abbot of the Cloud Temple Monastery."

"I am he." Claudian stiffened. "I c-cannot go."

The horseman stopped a few yards from Claudian and stirred uneasily in the saddle. "The Pontifex knows you, Claudian, that you will not obey a direct command, not even from him, if it does not suit you. But the matter is important. The Pontifex has been attacked by dark forces, and a devilish fever now troubles him."

Claudian took a step backward. "A shadow. A fell disease," he muttered. "A s-sign of the first End; and the second End shall follow s-swiftly after."

"I don't know what you're talking about." The horseman trotted closer. "My liege thought you might refuse. You have ever been insolent, he says. I have a letter from him. It will explain the trouble in the wider world. Perhaps it will convince you to obey."

The horseman handed him rope-bound papers. Claudian took it in his old wrinkled hands and the horseman spared no more time for conversation; eyes darting around, he whitened, yanked his reigns and galloped off the way he had come. Clouds approached from the west, promising snow or perhaps just ill omen. Claudian wondered why the messenger had been so afraid, why he had run off so quickly. Then he looked around him. Peaks of dark gray, capped with snow, surrounded this high valley; the mountains watched with dark eyes, some said. An initiate once dreamed a dark secret hid among those peaks, even wrote a poem in their honor: *There is a Shadow in the Vale.* Claudian had been through every inch of Cloud Temple, searched much of the valley, the scrub pineland, and climbed the peaks in the too-short summer. The growing dark spread, a shadow lived in the valley, and winter was coming.

1092

CHAPTER FOURTEEN:
THE LAUGHING GHOST

Pyoter Matheris, Hunter

The winter rains pelted Pyoter as he passed down the way. Steely gray clouds hung overhead, matching the monuments of Victory City—what once was Eximenius—a shrine to the dead, dedicated to the "god" Claudian Adamantus after he defeated the northern barbarians many decades ago. A garden of cypress trees, honoring the slain soldiers of the Empire, would no doubt enjoy the rain after the hot dry summer.

Pyoter shook the water off his wide-brimmed hat. The cold damp of winter, the near-omnipresent darkness, had turned his knees and joints sore and numb. A few yards past Victory City, a tavern advertised everything that Pyoter wanted on its outer sign: "SAINT LORANNA INN: Beds, Warm Fire, and Ample Food."

Inside, Yule wreaths hung on the walls and a bright fire blazed. In its light, a group of common citizens huddled, dressed in greens and reds, holding steaming cups of sweet Yule wine. Pyoter had forgotten the holiday was so near.

"Signore." The innkeeper walked up to him, a fat woman with a long blonde braid. "Shall I send a girl to take care of your horse?"

"My horse is dead." Pyoter should have stopped himself before he said the words. "Bandits, err— I shall not bother you with the tale."

The innkeeper frowned. "It is Yule eve, good signore. You shall not pay a single aes."

"I insist…"

"And I insist even more. A man waylaid by bandits, without a horse, shall not pay for lodging here. Else, the good St. Loranna would not smile upon us. It is Yule, for gods' sakes. You shall not pay. You shall not pay an aes!"

There are still good people left. Pyoter smiled wearily. "You are a good woman. Thank you."

"Have a seat by the fire, signore. You look dreadfully cold."

"I will."

"Some hot Yule wine will be right on its way."

Pyoter took a seat by the fire; the people there smiled and nodded graciously. Pyoter eyed the wooden floor, varnished and layered in beeswax. The inn had been built recently, within the last decade or so. As the warmth of the flame enveloped him, Pyoter remembered all that had gone on, the waylaying in the Central Valley. It had been a hot dry day, one of the last hot dry days before winter hit. A poisoned arrow struck his horse and the poison acted quickly; within a minute she had collapsed.

A group of men had appeared, dressed in dark blacks and grays, and asked, "Are you Pyoter Matheris, the Hunter?" They knew the agents of the Magisterium had sworn an oath never to lie. When he answered with silence, the six men knew they had found their quarry, and went in to attack. In the end, the martial skills he learned as a hunter paid off, yet at monumental expense; he had used the last of his crystal bolts, bought at exorbitant price from the magicians of Kheroe, and the Pontifex would certainly not by another. The explosive barrage had destroyed the bandits—who were, almost certainly, demoniacs—but now the cabals would be more difficult to defeat, their shrines more difficult to demolish.

One of the Yule revelers was looking at him: a woman with light brown hair flowing down her red and green dress. "Signore, you look ill."

Pyoter could not meet her gaze. He had not spoken with another person in so long, he barely knew what to say. "Yes." But the warmth of the fire still had not thawed his chilled body, his sore joints.

"Where are you going?" the woman asked.

"Imperial City." He had no reason to worry about these Yule revelers, he was certain, and he did not fear them enough to be careful. He peered into the woman's brown eyes; they were warmer than the fire.

"Imperial City. Beware the Laughing Ghost," she said. "Rumor says there is a spirit that murders people in their homes. She is in the garb of a jester. Folk around the city say to never answer a knock on your door if you hear a giggle first."

The woman's voice had an edge of delight, and her mouth a faint but present grin; she told the story like she would a frightful tale to spend a wintry evening like tonight. But rumor often had basis in truth. Pyoter wondered if this tale had a nugget of reality, if this ghost were real or if, perhaps, the woman was a member of the demon cabals that filled Imperial City. "Tell me more about this." Pyoter put on a fake smile. Right now he was incapable of a genuine one. "A jester you say. A giggle."

"The spirit of a woman," she continued, "that once performed in taverns around Imperial City. She was murdered, however, and her ghost remains to torture the living. It is said a holy symbol on your door will keep her out, but I hear even that will not stop her." She laughed. "I'd keep indoors at night."

"In Imperial City, it's always wise to keep indoors at night."

"Indeed," the woman said, "but of late, it is even wiser. Paint the Hammer of Hieronus on your door, good fellow. I never saw the Laughing Ghost, but I know for certain she is real."

CHAPTER FIFTEEN:
THE ANCIENT ONES

Claudian Adamantus the God, Monk Militant

This vale has secrets, Claudian thought as he looked out his chamber window. The Cloud Temple Monastery, after all, had not been the first building on its foundations. An older ruin had been here, its shattered arches and snapped pillars hinting at an ancient people long-forgotten.

In the weeks since the Magisterium's messenger departed, Claudian had read his reports thoroughly. All bad news of course—an ominous silence on the southern border, discontent among citizens, an enigmatic and ineffectual sovereign—and all designed to ask Claudian to return to the lowlands. All designed to compel Claudian to return to the White Throne where he once sat. The Pontifex once delighted in having a devout man like Claudian serve as ruler of the Empire. But he had put that behind him and he would not return. The name Adamantus, in many ways, had been a curse, a hindrance to the ascetic life he wanted: a life dedicated to perfecting the body and the mind.

"Claudian."

The voice of Brother Luther startled him. Normally, he could hear a person approach long before they spoke. *Perhaps aging does affect me after all.* Claudian turned to face the much-younger brother, second-in-command in Cloud Temple Monastery. For all his youth he had been here far longer than Claudian; though forty, at most, Luther had trained as a monk since age fifteen, since he was barely a man and incapable of a beard.

"I sense you are troubled. What bothers you, brother? You have always kept silent except when it is necessary to speak—a good thing, certainly—but..." His voice trailed off, perhaps at Claudian's stern look.

"My wellbeing is not your c-concern, brother. Concern yourself with t-training the initiates. Concern yourself with—"

"I care about you, brother," Luther said. "Your wellbeing may not be my concern, but I care nonetheless. 'The heart of man is dark.' 'The shadow spreads.' It is good to fight evil, but it is not good to fight it alone."

His earnestness was clear. "Ah, Luther." Claudian smiled. He could not remember the last time a smile had touched his lips. "I am not sure if 't-troubled' is the right word. Perhaps *wary*."

"Wary of what?"

Claudian again turned to survey the high mountain valley where they lived, buried deeper and deeper with every snowstorm. He shivered. "What do you know of this place? Who lived b-before us here?"

"When St. Traber climbed the mountain, it was empty. There were no people here. There was only a ruin. He—"

"But *who*? Who l-lived here before us? There is a story behind every ruin. Every ruin was once a building. Sometime l-long ago, p-people lived here in the vale."

"I don't know," Luther said. "But there was an abbot before you…"

"Selmer."

"Selmer was troubled with night visions. He spoke of the 'Ancient Ones.' One night, at midnight, he left and never returned. Thank Hieronus you came, brother. I do not want you to meet the same fate. It would destroy me if you disappeared too. You are my brother, but you are also the father I never had, my best friend."

Claudian turned to regard the younger brother. He had perfected his body the most out of any in the monastery—perhaps more than even Claudian—but he had not yet perfected his mind. "Luther, do not worry. If I ever left, y-you would have Hieronus. And moreover you would have the initiates to teach and to bring up in the W-Way. You must not attach y-yourself to any mortal. We are not t-to marry, of course—but we are not to have a friend we love more than the Way, no allegiance we hold more than to Heaven."

"I wish I had half your strength."

"Ah, Luther, your strength is d-different. In ways you are stronger than me. But you must learn to control your emotion. 'There is no h-human bond strong enough to never break, for the heart of man is dark, and the world is wild, and b-before the light will come the dark shall cover all.'"

A shiver visibly passed over Luther, and his already pallid complexion whitened. "Do you mean to say you would betray me?"

Claudian frowned. "There it is again. D-do not concern yourself with mortal bonds. Against m-my b-better judgment I shall t-tell you—and truthfully—that you are m-my friend. But even that is a concern of the m-mortal world. In my c-commune each night I pray for your g-good. B-but no mortal bond should t-trouble you, friend."

The color returned to Luther's face. His grave expression vanished. Perhaps, he was happy with the answer. But that would only mean that Claudian did not instill the lesson in him well enough. It was a lesson he learned in psalteries and religious texts, but more acutely on the White Throne: *There is no one in this world you can trust.* It was difficult to tell Luther because—in truth—he did love his younger brother; he was a friend dearer to him than any worldly possession, and he could not, in a thousand years, imagine betraying him.

But their conversation hung heavy in his mind. Luther had spoken of the former abbot, and chilling as the story was, all Claudian could think about were the 'Ancient Ones' that inhabited the valley long ago. On their ruins the lowlanders had built this great edifice where Claudian and the monks underwent their vigorous training. And if the abbot Selmer truly did perish because of them, then it was Claudian's duty to understand who they were, and how to end their influence. *But perhaps*, he thought as he stared out into the swirling white land between the mountain peaks, *Selmer was only mad.* The isolated life of the mountains often did that to minds.

Even the tough ascetics of the Cloud Temple Monastery had an archive. St. Traber, whose mortal perfection had never been equaled, had said a physical body immune to common ills could not attain perfection without a keen mind. Thus, even in the snowy mountains high above Paladium, Claudian walked among rows and rows of books: grammars, mathematical texts, and histories alongside the traditional psalteries, hymnals, and a giant illuminated copy of the Book of Order. Memorizing verses had uses beyond practical application, St. Traber had said; it sharpens the mind, helps it overcome the obstacles of fear and temptation, as well as the wiles of magic. At the pinnacle of his life, in the early years of the Empire, he could overcome the strongest of swordsmen with only his bare hands, move with absolute silence and stealth through enemy lands; and when the ancient Queen of Haroon, Astarthe, tried to cast her spell over him, compelling him to forsake his vow of celibacy, her powers of magic had bounced off his mind like a pebble off steel.

More than Claudian's father could say, if the history books were true. Claudio-Valens Adamantus, the undisputed master of the world, had fallen to temptation against the Queen of Haroon. Father had a gift of magnetism, people said, and the winds of Fortune blew always at his back; but in ways he was weak. His temper had brought the nations to his feet, but in flesh he was weak.

How different I am from him, Claudian thought as he scanned the rows of books. Claudian had ruled from the White Throne for two decades, then abdicated in favor of Bathalomer Severus. In the vastness of Imperial City, and most especially in the vicinity of the White Throne, temptations abounded. As emperor, beautiful women would do anything to have you. Spice users abounded even in the hallowed halls of the Imperial Palace. Addiction and lust—two things the Order of St. Traber compelled you to avoid. And Claudian would not let the temptations distract him from his goal: mental and bodily perfection in service of Hieronus, Lord of Justice. When the temptations became too much, he had left the White Throne for good. He would never go back.

Eventually, winding his way through the archives, he found what he searched for: the personal diaries of the abbot Brother Luther had spoken about. He pried it from the shelf and shook off the dust. Then he opened the pages, slightly stiff and yellow with age, and carefully flipped his way through it. The binding had dissolved and many pages slipped toward the floor before he caught them. Still, page by page, he read the words of Brother Selmer, looking for items of note:

The boy Luther Oremis is promising. He is rustic, though, and unrefined, a shepherd from the highland. I shall do my best not to hold it against him, Hieronus aid me. He is far ahead of the initiates of his age in body, but significantly behind in emotion and mind.

Claudian smiled faintly. Not much had changed. He flipped through the pages, seeing much inconsequential text, glimmers of the late abbot's worries about troublesome initiates or minor doubts about the faith. But toward the end of the diary, an entry caught his eye:

Ever since I ventured to the lowest level I have been troubled by dark dreams. I have not had a good night's sleep in a week. I fear I have disturbed some latent presence. And though I wake up startled, I so badly want to visit the lower levels. Hieronus aid me to heed your warning. Hieronus aid us all.

Claudian had no idea there was a lower level. Another entry soon followed:

I dreamed of a child lost in the mountains. I dreamed of

people who perished here, or most frighteningly, people who lived on somehow, despite the snow and cold. Yet in the surety of dreaming I know they are not good. Moreover, they are ancient… they are the ancient ones who lived in the mountain before us, on whose ruins Traber built the temple.

The hairs on the back of Claudian's neck stood on end, and a chill spread over his skin. He braced himself as he read the last entry:

I cannot resist my thirst for knowledge. I must return to the lower levels. I must find out the nature of these Ancient Ones. In my dreams I hear a man's voice at the secret door, saying 'Come, and hear my tale.'

Claudian backed away. He turned to exit the archives and begin his search for the secret door, the way to Cloud Temple Monastery's lowest level, where Selmer had lost his life.

"G-gods rest your soul, Selmer," Claudian breathed.

Brother Luther stood there in his habit. "Selmer did not die. He left the monastic life of his own will."

"Come with me on my journey, brother."

Luther's face lit up with a smile. "Nothing would make me happier."

Together, they would find the secret door. Together, they would find where the abbot Selmer went, and discover the truth of the Ancient Ones.

CHAPTER SIXTEEN: WELCOME PARTY

Tiverio Lucullus, Maestro of Foreign Affairs

From a land of stinging sand and dust, Lucullus and his century entered a land of natural gold pillars and deep canyons, following a steadily ascending road. The road itself had worn down to mostly dirt and loose pavestones; the padisha had neglected to maintain what once had been a heavily-traveled thoroughfare. The sun baked them at its highest point; they were a few hours from the golden plains of Fharas when a thunderous galloping echoed through the desolate land. In an instant, a dozen riders in loose white clothing and giant scimitars barreled onto the road.

The legionaries drew shields and swords. But the riders did not strike.

One, wearing a blue headband, shouted in Fharese: "Do any of you speak the High Tongue?"

"I do," Lucullus answered. None could serve as a maestro of foreign affairs without the ability.

"Northerners, obviously," the rider continued. "We do not come to harm you. In fact, we mean just the opposite... to prevent you from harm. The Great Lord Mirza offers you his protection and counsel."

Lucullus looked around to the legionaries. They did not have much choice.

~

The Great Lord Mirza and his subjects lived within a rock fortress carved from stone. On a raised throne sat the man himself, wearing a thin turban. A thin beard came to a point. Gems, inset on his brilliant orange robe, gleamed in the torchlight. All around him, his wives—six, Lucullus counted after a short glance around—wore green or blue lace veils, the Fharese sign of marriage. A woman wearing a veil was wed, and off-limits to a prospective Fharese man; a quite practical arrangement, Lucullus mused.

Lord Mirza's brown eyes held warmth and respect, but that did not help Lucullus' unease—the further south he traveled, the more uncomfortable he became. "Northerner," Lord Mirza said. "We have not seen the likes of you in many years. You will find the Stone People more welcoming than those on the High Plain. They bear no especial ill will to the northerners—no more than they always have—but they are troubled. I am sure you have heard…"

"I have heard little, Lord Mirza," Lucullus answered.

"The Dark Horde has poured in from the eastern plains, destroying everything in their path. Those who do not obey their onerous rules to the letter are sentenced to die. The people must submit to their god Mazda and reject all other allegiances except to him and the Theomancer. And what's more, you have a welcome party waiting for you. A few warriors of the Dark Horde know a band of northerners is coming."

Lucullus drew in a cold gasp.

"The Great Lords of Fharas are unanimously opposed to the Dark Horde, and the great padisha emperor himself has done everything he can to defeat them. But their martial skill is strong as their minds are uncultured. I warn you, northerner, not to take the open road. The legions are strong but the Dark Horde is stronger. I counsel you, Lucullus, to rest here for the night, have some rose-water and bread, and then we will lead you all by a safe route into the High Plain."

"I wonder how in Varda they knew we were coming," Lucullus said, more to himself than anyone else.

But Lord Mirza answered. "It seems the Theomancer knows all things… *sees* all things. There is no surprising him. He anticipates every move we make. It is the source of their victory. The High Magus suspects he has made a pact with shadow. Some magi have defected to the Dark Horde's side in their desire for wealth or material gains, claiming Mazda is the only true god… When a magus defames Athra Lord of Fire, and all the beings of Heaven, it causes the people to lose hope." Mirza had become enveloped in his own thoughts, ignorant of the original question. "But seeing those who live under the thrall of Mazda, their utter lack of joy and slavery to the Theomancer, many people of the kingdom would rather fling themselves into battle in a last stand than suffer years and decades under their unnatural laws."

It is evident that he has conviction, Lucullus thought. But in all, this conversation made him regret venturing this far south, obeying the emperor's commands. He had nothing to gain from this fight, and everything to lose.

"The padisha emperor will welcome your presence," Lord Mirza went on. "He has sent many letters to your nation—by land and by sea—and has not received any response. He worries that somehow the Dark Horde is intercepting them along the border."

Lucullus eyed the stone floor. "Our emperor…" He wondered if he should condemn Severus in front of all the legionaries. "…I sometimes wonder if he has sound judgment. I have said as much, that the enemy that troubles you may be fiercer than—"

"He has received them?" Lord Mirza cried and shot to his feet. "Old hatreds die slow." His voice in an instant lost its fire. "Old wounds take time to heal. I should have expected this. Your emperor must not have sound counsel. He will not see reason. We must end our war, Imperial. We must put aside our petty struggles. There are more precious things at stake than our pride. The war has weakened the Land of Fire. The Four-Pointed Star no longer flies as high. We tried so hard to defeat the north—the ones we should have held close as brothers—and in our efforts we weakened ourselves, while an enemy viler than any the world has ever seen pours into our borders… a millstone around mankind's neck, a heavy burden on the back of the world. The nomads who had nothing have come to destroy everything. Unchecked, they will lay waste to the world. Athra save us. Athra help us."

"Gods help us indeed," Lucullus breathed. He could see what Emperor Severus could not: an ally in the land they once hated, a friend kept at bay by old prejudices. "I will do all I can to help you. I will make an exhaustive report… a report so detailed our ruler will have no choice but to help you. The Empire still has its old strength. I pray to the gods we will use it in the proper way. Our emperor…" Lucullus bit his lip to avoid insult. The emperor deserved respect, even though it was Severus. "I will do the best I can, Lord Mirza. You have my word."

"We will all do our best." Lord Mirza eyed the floor, overcome with thought. "We Stone People have the best circumstances of all the Fharese. To you, our land is a maze of canyons. But we know all the twists and turns by heart."

"We should get some rest," Lucullus said. "I thank you, Lord Mirza, for your generosity and kindness."

"Do not thank me yet." Lord Mirza smiled. "I have another gift for you… an ally. Sidathra?"

Out of one of the stone corridors a man emerged, and Lucullus knew, in an instant, the man's profession. Sidathra stepped into the throne room: a tall southron man with an ash-gray beard and a lily-white turban, wearing long robes of purple and leaning on a shepherd's crook. His skin had the tone of brass. Sidathra was a magus, a worshiper and wielder of flame. "It is good to meet you, signore," he said in the Imperial tongue.

The magi are scholars, Lucullus remembered, *and it should not surprise me that Sidathra speaks many languages.* "It is good to meet you as well," he said. "I am Lucullus… *Tiverio* Lucullus, though everyone calls me by my surname."

A wide yellow smile spread across Sidathra's face, and he bowed so deeply it was a wonder he did not topple over. When their eyes met once more, he said, "I think we shall work well together. The padisha emperor will most certainly welcome your presence. He is in the summer capital and it is wintertime… a sign of desperation, certainly. I see you have not prepared adequately for the mountain cold. I will have Lord Mirza provide you with proper clothing."

Lord Mirza bobbed his head politely. "They shall have ample clothing and more. Though I hear the conjured flame of the magi heals like nothing else."

"The fire of Athra should never be used lightly," Sidathra chuckled. "You, a Great Lord, should know that best of all."

The joy vanished from the Lord Mirza's face. "Prepare yourselves… Lucullus, Sidathra, and you soldiers. The Southern World is at war. Take them to the summer capital, Sidathra, and be careful, all of you. The creed of the Dark Horde is no mercy. They have nothing to offer the world except violence, but they will destroy us if the northerners do not help."

They left in the early morning, led on by a few light cavalry and the magus Sidathra, riding on a thin white horse. They broke free from the canyons and rock-pinnacles before the sun reached noon. There, on the High Plain of Fharas, the golden grass stretched into the horizon. In the baking sun, Lucullus tugged at his collar.

Lucullus couldn't imagine how miserable the plain would be in summer. But here he was, at last in the Southern World. Nothing green lay in view except for a stand of junipers nearby. But a mile away, smoke wafted into the air, tarnishing the otherwise clear blue sky.

"A raid, most likely," Sidathra began. "A cattle-farmer's house, burning. When you know the raiders, you expect little from them."

But in the shadow of the smoke column, dark shapes formed, racing across the golden hills.

Lucullus kicked his heels into his horse's side, but Sidathra raised his hand and yelled, "Stop!"

The horse nickered at the retracted command.

"The raiders are swift. They will overtake us. Draw swords and shields. The best way to escape these dogs is to destroy them." The magus extended his shepherd's crook. The air around him wavered with heat, yet at the same time grew colder.

Lucullus gulped. A hard lump had formed in his throat and his hand trembled slightly as he drew his standard-issue Imperial blade. He dismounted; his horse was not meant for war.

At last, they were near. The horsemen wore loose clothing and black hoods, with a strip covering their mouths. The long sleeves of their robes blew behind them as they galloped, and it dawned on Lucullus that they had bows in their hands and quivers full of arrows on their backs.

Horse archers, he realized, and cursed himself for dismounting.

Then a horseman shouted something in their tongue—faint, because of the distance—and in concert they wheeled around to gallop due east. "They are going to tell the others!" Sidathra snapped, and in an instant the cold heat of his magic increased a hundredfold. A fireball blasted from his hand and seared a patch of dry grass, which immediately began to burn in a pillar of flame. Another conjuration— a lance of fire, sent spewing from his hand—missed a horseman by a hair's length, doubtlessly singeing his hood.

"Curse you magi!" Lucullus growled and heaved himself back on-saddle, preparing to gallop away by himself if need be.

But then Sidathra lifted his hands, and a wall of brilliant flame burst into existence where the horseman meant to go. They stopped themselves. *A mistake,* Lucullus thought. And Sidathra called up another wall of flame, then two more in a single motion, boxing them in.

I underestimated him, Lucullus realized.

Then Sidathra raised his hands high. He had saved the best fire-show for last. A pillar of flame filled in the square of fire, and even a hundred yards away, Lucullus heard—and enjoyed—their desperate screams.

"I underestimated you," Lucullus voiced his thought.

"So many do." The magus' skin looked more than ever like molten copper. His eyes gleamed with joy, then turned to regard the spreading flame. "The grass is dry in Gor Ilán," he said, "and I could quiet the wildfire if I wanted. But the enemy is near, and the good folk have likely fled. I will do whatever there is in my power to hinder them." The magus pulled the reins of his horse and touched the shepherd's crook to his heart. "I think we will get along well, Signor Lucullus."

"As do I," Lucullus answered. "As do I."

CHAPTER SEVENTEEN:
BLACK SHIPS

Astarthe

When she was a little girl, Issachar would tell her that one day her rose would bloom, her body bud into a full woman. She had argued with him, wondering how he—a Godling priest that only dressed in women's robes—could know. And he had struck her for her disrespect. But now, as she watched the waves foam in from the shore of the Isle of Birds, Astarthe realized he was right. In the months since she wedded her brother, she had grown in places she never thought she would, and underneath the weathered robe she wore, hair grew, hair that embarrassed her somehow. And Anakh... Anakh remained her lover, though even now she wondered if it was right.

Often, when she watched the whitecaps roll in from far away, she thought of the merling witch, Zaira, who had saved her family from the vicious Sea Raiders. She could never repay her. Captain Izeem had been so deathly wrong that merling witches hunted all humans; in the end it seemed that their grudge only lay against the Sea Raiders, or wicked folk in general.

Or perhaps, she thought. *Perhaps she just liked* me.

But the thought was vain, and vanity was dangerous to a refugee, Issachar said. *Issachar*, she thought, as she heard his steps approach in the sand.

"Do you see?" the Godling priest asked. "We have visitors."

Months had passed without a single ship; the rainy season had come and gone, and they had remained alone. Yet as Astarthe focused her eyes beyond the whitecaps, faint traces of black caught her eye. A dozen or so ships made their way toward the coast of the Isle of Birds... ships with lateen sails, colored black like pitch. "Where is Anakh?" she gasped. "He would know what to do."

While Issachar had all the physical qualities of a man, only

Anakh was brave. Even now, he was probably in the jungle, hunting. *The Sister-Queen,* Issachar once said, *is a shaper and weaver of emotion and wills. The Brother-King is a warrior and most importantly a hunter.*

"Anakh," Issachar breathed. "I will go get him."

Anakh

Spear in hand, Anakh leapt over a downed log and onto the dry rocky ground leading up the mountain. The monkey bounded away from him toward the undergrowth but Anakh continued his breathless pursuit. Like his sister he had grown, but he had grown in physical strength and stamina. Most days he provided the meal, and there were few animals that could outrun him.

"Anakh!" Issachar's voice rang out. "Anakh!"

Even still he hated that Godling priest.

"Anakh!"

The monkey slipped through the brush, disappearing into a wall of vines and leaves. Anakh cursed.

"We are in danger!"

Anakh slammed his spear onto the hard rock, ready to strike something in frustration. The Godling priest had distracted him like always.

"Your sister is in danger!"

He perked up, grabbed his spear even as it clattered across the ground, and ran toward Issachar's voice. The damned Godling knew how to get his attention.

He met his beautiful sister on the beach, and when he looked out into the sea, he saw what startled her: ships with triangular black sails, pushing through the ocean waves. Dhows, he realized, but most certainly not Fharese. Anakh had never seen a Fharese ship with a black sail. Sea Raiders often had black sails, but there was something about these he could not account for, something different about them.

Whatever happened, he knew he would be ready. He touched the cold of the metal spear to his bare chest. "Atman," he whispered to the god of the sun, his father. "Let my blows strike hard and fast, and guard me from compassion."

"Quiet," Issachar intoned. He turned his painted face to regard Anakh. "We must be wise. You are strong, Anakh, and will—as best I can tell—outdo your father. But you have a temper, and if you let it reign you unchecked it may spell your end."

Sometimes, Anakh wanted to spear him.

Issachar gazed at Astarthe, and for some reason the look he gave her stung Anakh with jealousy. "You are a woman, now," Issachar said, and the sting flared. "If it is in the interests of your safety, I permit you to use the power of *gleaming* as other queens before you have done. But you shall never do it to your brother or to me."

"I would never even dream of it."

"That is good." Issachar said, and within moments the ships had come within sight.

The men on the ships wore clothing as black as the sails. Around their heads they wore hoods, and around their mouths strips of black cloth hid their lips from view. When they jabbered to each other Anakh couldn't understand a word.

Issachar turned to them, pale. "They speak a tongue I barely know," he whispered. "The desert nomads, so far away… why are they here? These are strange times."

"Quiet," Anakh snapped, and when Issachar obeyed, he grinned. *Finally, he listens. He will learn to do that more often.*

Not far from shore, the ships landed in short order. The black-garbed men stepped out and splashed into the water. There were dozens, perhaps as much as a hundred. All of them had long steel scimitars. On a few black shirts Anakh noticed a serpent insignia, woven in silver thread.

One, holding two sabers, shouted something in his language.

One of his eyes was missing, Anakh noticed; perhaps plucked out in combat, or for past crimes. Whatever the reason, if he hurt Anakh's sister, he was dead. "I see you do not speak? What of the language of those Fharese dogs?"

"We do," Issachar answered.

"You do not speak the language of Mazda and his Most High Theomancer. We have looked all over for you. In his vision, the Most High Theomancer saw you on the Isle of Birds… two children, and a *thing*—a mockery of both man and woman."

Anakh gripped his spear tighter and pointed it outward.

"There are people who want you dead," the man went on. "But the Most High Theomancer has reasons for keeping you alive… for a while."

"You should not speak so rudely to the royal family," Issachar growled. "By rights these two belong on the Red Throne of Haroon. You should grovel before them, nomad."

Anakh paled. Even he knew Issachar had spoken rashly. For once he wanted restrain the Godling priest.

"The man-woman has a mouth," the black-garbed man snapped. "A lesser warrior would strike you dead. But instead I will do as I ought… obey the Theomancer's command. By the Law of Mazda, a man who dresses in women's garb should be emasculated and then set on fire."

Issachar took a step back and Anakh grew cold.

"That shall likely be your fate." The black-garbed man turned his eyes to Astarthe. They fixed upon her, examining her closely, and Astarthe pulled her clothing tighter. "If you are anything like the folk of Fharas, you have likely lost your flower. By the Law of Mazda, a woman of no virtue cannot wed a man. You may fall upon a sword, or serve the Theomancer as his concubine."

"I will kill you if you touch her," Anakh snapped.

The black-garbed man's eyes fixed on him. "You." It was unsettling not to see his mouth, covered as it was by a black cloth, though he spoke audibly. "You will see the error of your ways. I sense in time you will become a great warrior of Mazda.”

"I will never," Anakh growled. "I will fight against you to my last breath."

The man's eyes narrowed to slits. "After all this I have not introduced myself. I am Zayad Jabbar, sent from the Most High Theomancer himself. I will look forward to transporting you to him. The journey will be long. I hope you do not get too comfortable. I doubt you will." He turned to his lackeys. "Shave the man-woman, and force him out of that dress. Remove his face-paint and give him man's clothes. We will not defile the ship with an abomination."

"No," Issachar snapped. "No… Sacrilege…"

Anakh looked away as a man approached with a razor, ready to force Issachar into submission and cut his long hair. He thought of darting in, striking the man down as he approached. But he gulped and only tightened his hands around the shaft of his spear. He could not overcome these dozens of warriors, though even now he could feel the rage simmering inside him, the hatred Issachar had told him to use as a weapon in battle. He thought of the only parent he knew—a Godling priest, considered a monstrous thing by many—and couldn't help the tears forming in his eyes as the warrior cut off Issachar's hair. It was as if they were cutting away Issachar's very soul, killing Anakh's childhood.

He embraced his sister-wife, clutching her shoulders, and let the tears fall.

CHAPTER EIGHTEEN:
CABAL

Pyoter Matheris, Hunter

Pyoter entered Imperial City for the first time in years. He passed underneath the Arch of Conquest and entered the ancient hive of humanity, its streets densely packed even in the midst of a winter rain. He had spent so long in the Magisterium and the staid, outwardly pious land of Paladium that he had forgotten the world outside. On the brick face of an apartment block, a crude advertisement had been painted: a bare-chested woman reclining on a red couch, and the name of a brothel above her. Pyoter instantly looked down, filled with shame and sadness for his countrymen. What priests of the Magisterium dared not speak of, the folk of Imperial City displayed boldly on the walls of their towering buildings, feeling none of the embarrassment it deserved.

Before leaving the St. Loranna Inn, Pyoter had shaved his moustache. He dared not give any demon cabals advanced warning of his presence; many associated Paladians with the Magisterium, rightly or wrongly. If possible he wished to surprise the New Moon Tavern cabal, come upon them with the suddenness of a storm, and bury them in a flurry of crossbow bolts. All demoniacs deserved to die. The trick was killing them before they killed you.

Pyoter scanned the busy street as water trickled off his wide-brimmed hat. There were Khazidees here, a rare sight in Paladium, their copper skin and jet-black hair unmistakable as they wandered by him, shivering and pulling cloaks tight around their small frames. By all accounts the harvest of the Khazan River had boded well this year. They might claim the tears of the goddess Issa properly watered the seed of the god Atman, a peasant superstition that the Pontifex and the White Synod denied. But the Imperial powers-that-be did not care what the common farmers of Khazidea believed about Heaven or the gods, as long as they remained content enough to work, and an Imperial governor sat upon the Red Throne of Haroon. The Empire relied on Khazidea, the renowned Breadbasket of the World, for most of its food.

Pyoter kept down the road. A man in the purple sash of the Imperial government stood on the street corner, handing out a loaf of free bread to a child in worn rags. The program of free bread relied solely on the harvests of the Khazan River, and it reminded Pyoter that even in Imperial City—a hive of prostitution, drunkenness, and avarice—the goodness of the gods still remained in many ways. Even in a world with people so wicked they worshiped demons, goodness remained in the hearts of many. It warmed Pyoter's heart, but then he remembered the words of a priest whose name he could not remember: *Before the light will come, the dark shall cover all.* It was a grim reminder that things would get worse before they got better, that perhaps his fight in all was in vain in the full view of history.

Perhaps, Pyoter thought, *I am just wasting my time.*

Eventually the rain stopped, and the sun peeked through receding clouds. Pyoter found himself in the Market District where he had intended to go all this time. There, a cobbler shouted about the fine shoes and sandals he had made; an artisan displayed her whalebone statuettes to passersby; and a tailor began laying woolen tunics out on his table, taking advantage of the dry weather. But there was something else: rumors, whispered to one another amidst the noise. More than once, Pyoter heard the word "Pontifex" and that more than anything else sent a chill up his spine.

Trouble in the Magisterium, he thought. *Right after I left?*

Trumpets pealed. Imperials looked toward the High Podium where official announcements of the court were made. Pyoter made his way over there. Standing behind a lectern, flanked by two red-cloaked members of the Imperial Guard, a white-garbed man with a purple sash began to speak.

~

"There are many lies being spread about the current catastrophe in Paladium!" he shouted.

A lump formed in Pyoter's throat.

"The Pontifex has taken deathly ill, yes! His malady is life-threatening, yes! He is covered in boils, yes! But there are no 'moglins' or 'grumps' flying around the spires of the Magisterium, and 'the end' is not near. There is no reason to panic! Emperor Severus has generously donated nine-hundred gold libra for his quick recovery, and he has sent the best physicians Imperial City can offer! The emperor asks all citizens and subjects of the Empire to pray to the gods for the Pontifex's swift healing. Those able to make a sacrifice should do so! By the light of Heaven, Emperor Severus proclaims, the Pontifex will once again be well and shepherd the Imperial flock. Do not worry! All will be well!"

Yet those were only words.

~

Down the street, Pyoter walked, looking for "The New Moon Tavern."

On a street corner a group of youths in black woolen tunics talked amongst themselves. "The Pontifex deserves what he got," one said. "He is a seller of lies, designed to comfort the weak…"

"I don't know, Gordo. That's a bit—"

"Theiarchus would have said the same."

Pyoter bit his lip and restrained himself from stepping into the conversation. Theiarchus, the founder of Thenoan Philosophy, called the gods abstract concepts to comfort the weak. A small wonder, considering Theiarchus was the most privileged, bluest-blooded nobleman to ever live. He knew nothing of life.

Restraint, Pyoter cautioned himself. But he could not help glaring at the young men as he walked by.

~

Eventually, as the day warmed and the sun reached its highest point, Pyoter laid eyes on the New Moon Tavern, nestled within a narrow street. The center point of the Imperial City cabals, or at least *an* Imperial City cabal. He bit his lip again, and couldn't help but admit his nervousness. He had done the exact thing many times before, but this was someplace new. Paladium was, and always had been, his home. But he gathered his courage and forced himself inside.

Inside the nondescript tavern, a large hulk of a man with blond hair stood behind a desk. "Greetings traveler," he said. "Welcome to the New Moon. I am Barto Aldera."

Or Black Snake, Pyoter wondered.

CHAPTER NINETEEN:
THE SEARCH

Claudian Adamantus the God, Monk Militant

A secret door in Cloud Temple Monastery. Claudian Adamantus had never expected such a thing, but Brother Luther—searching alongside him—had made no doubts that Selmer had not lost his mind, that if he wrote of something it surely existed. Brother Luther followed him a step behind. Claudian was like a father to Luther, though to Claudian, Luther was a brother under their common father, the god of justice and just war, Hieronus. In the early morning, as the initiates had just begun their daily exercises after a meal of bitter roots, Claudian and Luther looked through each room of the lower level, wandering through the plain corridor of stone. Winter had fallen over St. Traber's Vale, and the monastery—bereft of heating—had grown cold enough to sap the strength and eventually kill a non-monk. But neither Claudian nor Luther, dressed as they were in light woolen habits, so much as shivered.

"I w-wonder what Selmer found," Claudian mumbled as he and Luther searched through a storeroom. Here there were only cleaning supplies: piles of lye soap, buckets for water, and old rags.

As part of their training regimen, Claudian made sure they kept Cloud Temple Monastery clean. Cleaning might not seem good preparation for life as an ascetic warrior, but Claudian knew that cleaning—especially such a large complex as the monastery—developed patience and discipline as much as any hand-to-hand technique or strenuous exercise. A country farmwife, managing her household and ensuring its cleanliness, worked just as hard as her husband out in the fields. As he did his last scan of the room, Claudian thought of his mother Anthea—Anthea the Divine, as some erroneously called her—but he staved off all thoughts of her. He had never truly known about her; she had, after all, sent him to train as a monk at a young age because she thought him mentally unfit. But he had forgiven her. And besides, to a militant monk of the Order of St. Traber, there was no bond to value more than your union with the god Hieronus. To Claudian, there was no mother nor father; no friend nor enemy. He only had one goal: the perfection of body and mind in the service of Hieronus.

They kept down the stone passageways, searching briefly through rooms that the monks rarely visited. The further and lower they got within the winding corridors of the Cloud Temple Monastery, the more abandoned and ill-tended the bland stone rooms became. Silent, like all monks, all sound faded. There was complete silence… except tapping beneath them.

It wasn't truly a tap, more a scraping or a scratch. In fact, the noise was so faint Claudian—an instant after he heard it—determined he had only imagined it. But when he looked back to Brother Luther, he had assumed a battle-ready stance, each foot and hand ready to strike.

"You heard it too?" Claudian whispered.

Luther bobbed his head. Slowly, his muscles relaxed. Claudian turned and headed further down the hallway, eyes scanning for secret doors. They did not hear the noise again.

~

An hour passed, and Claudian lost track of where he had gone and which halls he had seen before. The basement of Cloud Temple Monastery was a maze, it seemed. At some point he lost track of time, having no idea whether it was day or night. He removed a torch from a sconce and instructed Luther to do so as well. Soon they came to a part of the lower levels where the torches had burnt out, standing forgotten for weeks or months or decades on the sconces where they'd been last lit. A sign that Claudian neared his goal, the secret door where he would learn all there was to know about the fate of Selmer, and the "Ancient Ones" he had searched for.

"S-Selmer," Claudian muttered as he peered through the musty, forgotten rooms along a more and more disheveled corridor, across rougher and rougher flagstone. "I wonder what happened t-to him."

"I said I saw him!" Brother Luther snapped. His harsh tone was not due to malice, Claudian knew; the trembling in his voice proved it was fear. "He lived. He left the monastic life. He joined the laity, left the order…"

Claudian let his voice trail off. If he argued or used harsh words toward his beloved brother, it would only worsen his fear. *Ah,* he thought, *a brother who could defeat a knight with just his bare hands, rive his iron plates of armor in twain, and yet has such poor command of his emotions…* It was sad that his gifts were so imbalanced. A living weapon, Brother Luther was, but an unsteady one. It did not help that the air was growing colder. Even Claudian—the highest-ranked monk of St. Traber—had begun to shiver.

~

Through the corridors they wandered for undetermined time. Then Luther spoke.

"Brother."

Claudian turned to regard him. Luther was pointing ahead— to the wall ahead, where the corridor stopped in a dead end. Claudian focused his eyes, and made out a circular line running across it: the imprint of a secret door, perhaps. He would find out. "You impress me, brother. I did not notice." Claudian approached the door and felt around it for a handhold. Dust fell off, revealing abstract patterns, indentations and symbols he did not recognize. He pushed, and sparks flew; they would have burnt his hand if he did not draw back suddenly, dodging the electric lash. "A magic d-door. I would guess there is s- some phrase, a password."

"A phrase we are not likely to ever learn."

Luther spoke truth. "You are right, brother."

"Step to the side, brother."

Claudian looked back at Luther. He was backing away. Claudian knew what he was trying to do. A difficult and dangerous proposition, but if anyone could do it, it was Luther. "Luther, I caution you…"

"Do not caution me," Luther said. "I did not wander all this way to find the secret door, only to be stopped by it."

"Perhaps Hieronus does not want us to go, brother."

"We will see, won't we?" And with that, Luther charged. Each bounding step took him several feet and then, drawing in a breath, he nailed the magic door with a flying kick. Lashes of electricity burst from it like a lightning storm, but Luther's aim was true. The door burst open in a cloud of dust; Luther flew into the room and landed, undamaged. There was a faint scream and he was gone.

Claudian rushed forward, leaping over the sparking, coruscating magic door in its death throes, and when he landed on the dirt floor it gave out beneath him like it had given out for Luther.

~

Claudian held his breath as the thin floor of dirt and rock crumbled and then swallowed him. He fell through the floor and ice shattered above him. In his breathless free-fall the dirt floor of the forgotten room gave way to a chute of solid ice. He landed on his feet several fathoms below on a floor of ice, slipping for a moment but catching himself. The impact would have killed a non-brother. Brother Luther stood a few yards away, balancing precariously on the icy ground. Icicles hung above on the high ceiling; ice caverns led in every direction. And now Claudian knew for certain he had not heard the noises. Now, the chittering echoed through the vast empty vaults, putting Claudian's training to the test—his blood ran cold with fear as he realized, *We are not alone.*

CHAPTER TWENTY:
WINTER IN THE SUMMER CAPITAL

Tiverio Lucullus, Maestro of Foreign Affairs

In a land where the enemy could see all things, it was only a matter of time before they found you. But as Lucullus soon learned, the magus Sidathra offered a sort of protection against him. A talisman, he said, made from what looked like white crystal, which blocked the Theomancer's all-seeing eye. Still, they were not protected from the non-magical detection of the raiders. And those very raiders traveled the sunbaked golden grass of the High Plain with dangerous frequency. Throughout their journey east, a day did not go by without sighting the pillaging servants of "Mazda"—a column of horse arrayed in black, ready to assault and raze a town to its foundations. That, Sidathra said, was the punishment for rebelling against their dark god's unnatural law.

~

About a week after they had left the protection of the Stone People and Great Lord Mirza, the rolling High Plain gave way to a rapid drop-off. They traveled down several switchbacks, descending the plain's elevation alongside the rock wall. Eventually a river appeared… swiftly flowing, wide and impossible to bridge. Beside it lay a land of dry rock and sand, but at the shore was a ferry.

"No foreigner believes me when I say this," Sidathra said, turning back to face Lucullus. His white turban was positively radiant in the burning sun. "This river… you know it as the Khazan."

"No…" Lucullus couldn't believe it. The Khazan created greenery and life wherever it went. "The land is barren here."

"But you can thank this water for all your grain." Sidathra's expression grew pensive, cold. "The grain you stole from us."

Lucullus thought of what he could say. In the end he made no answer.

~

A trip across the river, and their small band once more made an ascent up switchbacks—this time, a lower altitude, but still quite taxing to their horses. The ground above was rockier, with less grass. And far east, Lucullus could make out—through the burning haze—the shadow of a great peak. The mountains were approaching, he realized.

Through the barren country of red earth, grass, and twisting thorns, the journey continued several more days. The mountains appeared, mountains like the giant, impossibly tall ranges in the east of Eloesus. *Perhaps*, Lucullus thought, *they are one and the same*. But as a child Lucullus had been given a most unfortunately incompetent geography tutor. Few knew the layout of the Southern World, ever since Emperor Severus closed the border, forbidding anyone but unarmed merchants to enter. Now, with the widespread tumult, even those were rare.

Eventually, the pines began and Lucullus found himself in a silent red-earthed land in the mountains' shadow. Small birds fluttered through the trees, and every so often a deer would sprint across the old mountain path. So, too, did they find the remains of camps dotting the road—piles of ash where the communal fires had been, disturbed earth where huntsmen or refugees had walked or ridden. And slowly but steadily, the mountains took shape; great stone giants, reddish-gold and covered with pines for most of their extent. So tall were they that snow crowned the tops, even despite the blazing, ungodly heat where Lucullus and his century rode.

He could not imagine how tall the peaks before him were; but if anyone needed a respite from the horridly hot summers in the

Southern World, Lucullus could not imagine a better place—and that, after all, is where they rode. To the summer capital where the padisha emperor had once hunted and enjoyed himself, but now where he remained in hiding, his lands all but stolen by the Theomancer and his dark, destructive army. Not for the first time, Lucullus prayed for the padisha's safety and eventual triumph. But—as he remembered what he had seen before—he wondered if that was too tall an order even for the gods.

The dirt road wound its way up the mountainside. Pools of water and mountain streams gave Lucullus and his men no end of relief from the dry sun. But little by little the sun's power faded; the air grew colder, thinner, as they continued into the high country. At night, Lucullus was cold as he ever remembered being, and occasionally on a wet day, snowflakes would moisten and turn to water on his skin as he slept.

~

On the fourth day of their climb, a group of outriders passed them by, bow and arrow in hand. When their eyes met Sidathra's, they lowered their weapons.

One spoke in the Fharese tongue: "Friends. The godly sovereign of all Fharas, King-of-Kings, the Well-Born, the Beloved-of-His-Father, the great padisha Pharzanes bids you welcome." His tone lost some of its suspicion when he stopped the ceremonial blabbering. "A magus, I see, bearing the magic pendant." He switched to the Imperial tongue. "And northern friends as well. Greetings, legionaries. Has the emperor finally sent you?"

"In a way, yes," Lucullus answered him, and he did not know what he meant. "My soldiers are eager to meet the King-of-Kings and do what we can to aid him."

A smile touched the man's tan face. He stuck his arrow back into its quiver. "Follow the road," he went on. "I'm sure the magus knows the way." Together, the Fharese warriors galloped off, up the steeply-ascending road.

Lucullus and the soldiers rode on. "When you see Pharzanes, prostrate yourselves. It is humiliating, perhaps, but it is the Fharese way."

"I will not!" one legionary growled, and Lucullus smiled.

Of all the southrons' stereotypes about Imperials, their disrespect for monarchs was the most accurate. The centurion Valentus answered the insubordinate: "You will honor the Fharese emperor if I demand it, and I do." He paused, perhaps turning to Lucullus. "How shall we know which one is Pharzanes?"

"The padisha emperor wears a gold neck-brace to 'stretch his head toward the Heavens,'" Lucullus said, recalling history books and the war-diaries of Claudio-Valens Adamantus. "That should give his identity away if you are a fool and can't tell by his giant throne."

No legionaries laughed, perhaps because the jab had been directed toward their superior.

"Things have changed in Fharas," Sidathra said, riding a few yards ahead. "You shall see for yourself soon. Some things have changed because of the Dark Horde, yes; but much has changed because of Claudio the Destroyer… the one you call god."

A *god*, Lucullus corrected him silently, *if even that*. After all, not everyone took his divinity seriously, especially not in Anthania and Gad, where temples to Claudio-Valens and the Adamanti were forbidden. Still, it would be interesting to see how things had changed, how Claudio-Valens Adamantus—god, human, or devil—had transformed the land he invaded almost a hundred years ago. The respect, positive or negative, the Fharese had for Claudio reminded Lucullus there was potential for friendship, if Emperor Severus could open his senile eyes to see it.

~

By the time they reached the padisha emperor's hideaway, it was easy for Lucullus to see why the area was a summer and not a winter capital. Even by day, the sun reflected coldly on them, the air was thin, and patches of snow lay sporadically among the pines.

Soldiers—Fharese natives, judging by their long black beards and huge scimitars—filled what was once a pleasure retreat. A handful of magi in white turbans wandered around, each wearing the same crystal talisman that Sidathra wore. Looming above them all was what could only be the padisha's ancient retreat, a huge sprawling complex. *A log palace,* Lucullus mused. But nonetheless the sovereign of Fharas and the southern kingdoms remained outside with his troops.

The throne, hewn of dark gray stone, was covered with tiger-pelts and lion-skins up its many steps. At the pinnacle, the stone-backed chair bore the Four-Pointed Star of the southron empire. And sitting there was Pharzanes, looking nothing like Lucullus expected.

He was young, clearly, barely in his twenties at most. He had none of the strange trappings that previous padishas had of old—his neck had no brace, he wore no earrings or jewelry or face-paint—and in all he had no decorations except his robe. He wore his black hair short, and on his head he did not wear a turban or even a crown, but instead a thin brass circlet, as if he were trying to emulate the northern emperor.

His robe, however, was anything but plain. It fell halfway down the throne's many steps, made of silk and studded from bottom to top with fiery rubies, celestial sapphires, bright green emeralds. Gold thread wove through it, forming intricate patterns, and each foot of the fabric was a new color, forming the whole spectrum of the rainbow.

Lucullus knelt and fell face-first to the dry dirt. He heard Valentus and the legionaries follow a second later.

"Greetings, Pharzanes, great padisha, ruler supreme and chosen of Heaven…"

"Silence," Pharzanes answered him in the Imperial tongue. "Stand up."

Lucullus looked up in surprise, but Pharzanes' face was solemn and serious. Lucullus scrambled to his feet to obey.

"If we are to be friends, we must see each other as equals. Do you not agree?" Pharzanes said.

"I... of course," Lucullus breathed. He had expected change, but not this much.

"Does the emperor Severus grant me aid?" Pharzanes asked. "I have written to him many times, and received no reply. A messenger from him is much better than I expected. I feared he ignored my pleas, or worse."

"Worse?" Lucullus said.

"That he sees me as an enemy. Or that he aids the Dark Horde..."

"I assure you he does not... I am certain about the latter. He knows little about the Dark Horde, and the field reports are uniformly negative."

Pharzanes nodded. "Why have you come?"

"I came merely to make a report of the Southern World. I have risked death to meet you, Your Highness. It seems the raiders were well-aware of my coming."

"That does not surprise me in the slightest," Pharzanes said. A cold gust blasted into the valley and he drew his robe tighter; Lucullus bared his teeth and flinched. "The Theomancer sees all. The archmagus Adastra said he thinks the Theomancer is using some tool of sorcery... that was before the archmagus was betrayed. Even the magi capitulate, betray the cause of Athra Lord of Flame." Pharzanes looked glum. "But without my magi I would be dead, my kingdom lost. They have warded against the Theomancer's eye... I am safely hidden here."

"In the summer capital?" Lucullus stammered, a rude comment to the padisha in any other stage of Fharese history. "Surely they would know to search here... or send someone to search."

"Even in the golden years of our kingdom, the common folk did not know the location of the summer capital," Pharzanes went on. "It is no matter, though. Tell me how I can help you, northern friend. I apologize, I have been troubled the past few days... more so than most."

"Why, Your Highness?" Lucullus said. The conflict had gone on for months by now, probably years.

"I have had a terrible dream," Pharzanes said, "and none of my magi know what it means."

"Perhaps I can help you," Sidathra said, and trotted a few steps forward.

Lucullus remembered the magi—besides wielding flame—had a more important task, to interpret dreams. Among the Imperials, dreams were considered meaningless. But in the Southern World, he remembered, every dream was a riddle, a key to seeing the future. Lucullus wondered which approach was right.

"I dreamed of a statue of silver, forged in the shape of a man," Pharzanes said. "The statue, I knew, was very old. But a giant sword of crude iron struck it and nearly broke it in half; and then a great blue hammer smashed it to pieces."

A blue hammer, Lucullus thought to himself. *Adamant.*

"I do not know," Sidathra said. "But I will pray to the Lord of Flame, that he might shed his light on the matter."

Lucullus wondered if he knew the meaning... that the Dark Horde, an unworked, crude weapon of iron, dealt a harsh blow to Fharas—the brass statue—and then the Empire—the blue hammer of adamant—bashed it to pieces, dealing the death-blow. *Perhaps I should be his interpreter*, Lucullus mused. But if he was right, the truth was grim, and the exact opposite of what he wanted. The padisha emperor had been so good to him and all his men. *Our people could be friends, but Emperor Severus will not see it.* Not for the first time, he cursed that wizened old man.

"We are well stocked in provisions," Pharzanes said. His gloom seemed to have deepened. "I will make sure you are well-fed, and have for yourself whatever you require."

At night, the padisha's servants lit a fire in the grand hearth, which painted the log walls red and orange. Other servants brought out goblets of wine and loaves of bread. Lucullus took a seat near the padisha himself, and recorded what he said. After all, this was a mission of reconnaissance, and as soon as he knew all the goings-on in the Southern World, he could go back to Vera and his children. He knew they missed him, Vera most of all.

"East of Gor Ilán, east of even here, there is a great plain," Pharzanes said at one point in the night. "The horse peoples roam it and use it as a hunting-ground for the great beasts that dwell there. Beyond there, beyond even the Bay of Sur, the air grows drier and drier until you reach a great sandy desert, the Desert of Hamma. We knew little of what lived beyond there, only that impoverished nomads made a bare subsistence, surviving on deep below-ground wells and hunting what little game they could. But we underestimated them, as men often do. All the tribes of the Hamma Desert united, you see, under the Theomancer... a man who claims to be sent by god, which he calls Mazda. This was more than thirty years past. They pushed in from the east, going into the plain I spoke of—the wild plain of Megiddo—and a few embittered horse lords joined his cause. They made war on Sur, going all the way to the walls of Janshi. Others went across the plain and made war on the unbelieving horse lords. One by one the horse tribes swore allegiance to the Theomancer and called Mazda god. The tribes that did not believe were decimated one-by-one. They came to the Spice Cities to exact tribute. And that was when my father Khosrau first heard of them... I was barely a toddling child then.

"The lords of the Spice Cities—the Mercantors—have no use for honor or bravery. They paid off the nomads and the horse lords, let them build a shrine to Mazda and offered a monthly tribute. My father was enraged. He left south from Seshán, announced to the Great Lords that a levy was to be taken. All able soldiers would serve under him. He thought he would drive these nomads away quickly, make an example of the captives, and burn the Theomancer alive. But he was so wrong… so terribly wrong."

Lucullus furiously scribbled notes.

"The raiders are excellent riders. Whether horseback or camelback it did not matter… on the outskirts of the Spice Cities the enemy won their first victory. There was such a slaughter that when the Mercantor burned them, as is our custom, the pile stretched higher than the walls. Now the Mercantors are faithless, you see, and they went just short of pledging allegiance to the Theomancer, uncertain as they were of who the victor would be. The Mercantors strongly implied to the raiders that they were on their side; all while giving lip-service to the padisha."

"And what now?"

"The Mercantors continue to pay them tribute. They have all but joined with the Dark Horde," Pharzanes said. "But my tale is not over. Twenty years ago they crossed the river, ascended the High Plain of Gor Ilán, where the padishas have reigned in succession for eternity. When the border towns refused to pay homage to their god, they burned their buildings and stole their gold. It was the beginning of the end, we know now. But my father, despite all the travails that had befallen his kingdom, had no respect for these nomads—these 'people of the sandy waste who had nothing.' It was not until ten years later, when they leveled Seshán, broke the heads off all the statues they considered 'idols,' and removed—brick by brick—the Stepped Throne that surveyed the holy city like a mountain… it was only then that my father Khosrau realized his danger.

"He demanded the Pasha of Sur to send all his war-elephants and fighting men and elementalists, but for the first time in remembered history Janshi did not answer his call. Every battle he fought he lost. On the edge of the High Plain, in the midst of the wheat-fields, my father made his last stand. The raiders slew all his men—fifty thousand total—and broke through to the satrapy of Taifun. That was five years past. The satrap of Taifun remains loyal to me, the true padisha. The walls of Taifun are strong, and the archmagus thus far has held off the raiders encamped all around. The Greatest City in All the Worlds is safe for now, as far as I have heard. Their navy is strong. Our allies throughout the world supply it food. No one truly wants the yoke of the Dark Horde around the neck, not even the Mercantors who refuse to fight it. But the raiders are strong, and their leader the Theomancer sees all. Now, do you see why I am in hiding, Lucullus? Now, do you see why I need help? Claudio the Destroyer humbled us. His armies brought Archamenes back to your country for judgment, stole the Fertile Land from us. From my grandfather on we have not called ourselves the God-Kings. If your armies could defeat us out our most strong, perhaps the Dark Horde would fall to the Imperial legion. Don't you understand, now, that the land of Fharas is not your true enemy?"

Lucullus set his pen down. "I do." All around the feasting hall, the sounds of merriment echoed. His legionaries gulped down wine, shouting and laughing along with the Fharese men, like they were friends.

Perhaps we should be friends. He knew they should. But Emperor Severus… he exhaled. "If I were emperor, I would send the legions right away."

A weary smile touched Pharzanes' face. "Then you are a good man. I assume the my pleas have fallen on deaf ears."

"The emperor…"

The doors of the feasting hall flew open, and a man burst through—a soldier, likely, judging by his scale-mail armor and sheathed sword. "We have been betrayed! The magus Belastra has taken flight. But first he has dispelled our wards."

Lucullus' eyes met Sidathra. The once bright-white crystal had faded to a dull gray color.

"He is right!" Sidathra cried.

"So many traitors in our midst." Pharzanes did not sound surprised, only weary. "But those who convert to the Law of Mazda only do so for unholy reasons… for silver and gold, for license, for power or to save their wretched lives. We must move again. Perhaps we will head to Taifun. At any rate, our position is compromised. Will you come with us, good northman?"

"I… No." The words weighed heavy on him as soon as he spoke. But there was Vera his bride to consider, pregnant and in need. There were his children. "I will do my best to convince the Emperor Severus."

Pharzanes slumped in his chair, and his face relaxed, growing even further resigned. "May Athra guide you home. And may Athra save our country."

"I will say a prayer for you," Lucullus said. But before he prayed, there were further things to take care of.

When he told his plans to the centurion Valentus, his hard face did not change. He nodded. "We have done our duty to the nation. The emperor will be pleased. You have your notes?"

Lucullus nodded.

Sidathra was not nearly as open to the idea. "I will not go," the magus hissed. "The great padisha offers you food, wine. Even the gift of his presence is more than the common folk receive. To look upon him is permitted only to the Lords of Fharas. And you… you spurn him, abandon him in his darkest hour. If you go back to your nation, you will go alone. My place is with the padisha emperor, in Taifun the Greatest City in All the Worlds. I do not keep folk such as you for company."

"I am sorry," Lucullus said. And he meant it. But he was not sorry enough to abandon the image of Vera, large with child, needing him and already sick with worry.

Sidathra sneered. "Goodbye, faithless northerner. May Athra burn you to dust."

That, Lucullus thought, was harsh even for what he had done.

The god Athra, Lord of Flame and the Efreeti, would surely understand he had done his duty; that he had done just what his liege had told him. But he remembered that the Imperials did not care for Athra or his efreeti servants, and neither did Athra or his efreeti care for them. Instead, he said a prayer to Imperium, the Spirit of the Empire, and to Cadelara the Night Rider for swift travel. Then, with a nod to Valentus, he turned and headed for the door to leave.

CHAPTER TWENTY-ONE: THEOMANCER

Astarthe

They were eight days out to sea, with no land in sight. In the distance, thunderheads had formed. And Astarthe was screaming.

Not for herself, no. This had nothing to do with her. Two of those evil raiders that called themselves the lawgivers held her arms as she struggled. She screamed because Issachar, her father and her mother—shaved and dressed for the first time in a shirt and pants, a gangly masculine creature she did not recognize—was being thrown overboard.

"By the Law of Mazda a man who wears the garb of a woman must be killed," said Zayad Jabbar, the chief of the raiders whom Astarthe had grown to hate more than disease and death itself. "Does it surprise you, little witch, that Mazda has sent a storm to punish our failure to act?"

"Issachar is a good man! He is my friend!" Astarthe screamed. "Let him go, or... or..."

"Or what, little witch?" Zayad Jabbar said, and his eyes narrowed playfully. "Your power has no effect. You can do nothing but see the Law of Mazda enacted."

The fire of life had left Issachar's eyes; he was like a dead man. Nevertheless, he spoke: "Be brave, my king and queen! Stay strong to the end! May Atman guard you—"

Zayad Jabbar hurled him overboard into the sea. "Blasphemy!" he said.

The storm came anyway.

~

The lawgiver captain had spoken truthfully. Within the

confines of the ship, she could no longer touch the *gleaming* power within her. She could not affect the lawgiver's mind. She could not even calm herself. She had been many places, and endured many things, but never before had the air around her been so devoid of power, so empty. Zayad Jabbar had caused it; she knew that much, but no idea how. He did not seem like a sorcerer. He did not give off any of the telltale emanations. But perhaps that also was a mere symptom of the effect he created: a place devoid of power, of life, of joy.

The lawgivers knew how to torture her, as well. They had separated her from her husband and brother, Anakh. After killing the only parent she had ever known, they took her brother away from her. The cruelty was worse than the worst behavior of the Tiger Queen. At the thought of Issachar, shaven and paraded around the ship like a prize, then tossed into the sea, floundering for life, tears formed in Astarthe's eyes. For once she realized how much she loved her parent, how much—despite his strict rules and frequent punishments—he loved her. *Issachar loved me.* And she'd never see him again.

All around her the waves crashed and thunder roared over the shrieking winds. She wondered if it would be best that the storm took them, dragged them to the ocean bottoms, and drowned them all in the sea. The lawgivers deserved as much; but Issachar would not have wanted that.

Issachar. At the name she buried her head in her hands, and began to cry.

~

At least twelve days passed, and perhaps more—each more torturous than the next—before Zayad Jabbar showed his face again. His lackeys had been there before every so often to give her stale bread or a cup of water. To their credit they never tried to touch her, but that was the only good they did. She missed her brother Anakh. *Where is he,* she thought to herself. She glared into Zayad Jabbar's eyes.

He spoke, mouth covered by the strip of black cloth, a black hood covering his hair. "We are nearly to the Theomancer's camp. We have entered the Bay of Sur. Be ready, little witch. Clean yourself. The Theomancer does not like dirty girls."

"I will not do anything for you," Astarthe hissed. "I will try to look worse for your blasted Theomancer! I hope he dies!"

Zayad Jabbar glared at her for a few seconds. Then he rushed over her with the fury of a storm, striking her cheek with a balled fist and drawing up tears. He struck her chest, caused her tender breasts to shudder. She cried out in pain. "I teach you a lesson for your own good, witch," Zayad Jabbar hissed. "The Theomancer will do far worse to you if you treat him with a fraction of the disrespect you showed me. He nailed a hundred rebel villagers to wooden crosses for speaking against him. He will do far worse to a little witch." Zayad Jabbar made one last snarling face, then jerked away from her and stalked off, up onto the deck.

~

A few hours later, the ship stopped. The *caws* of birds and the shouting of people indicated they had come to a city, or at least a town. Astarthe bit her lip to quell the cold nervousness growing in the pit of her stomach, and the tears of fear forming in her eyes.

Anakh

Throughout the past two weeks, Anakh had helped Captain Zayad and the rest of the lawgivers sail, and it was nice to see their hard work pay off. They had come to a hot, dusty land called Bajir, with few trees and a lot of wide open spaces, but when they finally reached the Theomancer's camp, the dry grass had become pavestones, surrounded by a thick ash-gray wall.

When Anakh first saw the lawgivers kill Issachar, he hated the lawgivers as much as the padisha probably did. But slowly as he worked the sails, sweating and toiling along with them, everything started to make sense. It wasn't right for a man to dress in woman's clothing. Men should be men, and women should be women. Besides, for all the restrictions the lawgivers placed on women, there was no real problem if Anakh—a man—lusted after women. With the lawgivers there were different standards for men and women, and the standards made sense. Now, though still a bit reluctant, Anakh was eager to meet the Most High Theomancer for himself, and learn more about Mazda and his law.

In the center of the town—if you could call it that—a stone tower the same ash color of the walls stretched maybe one-hundred feet in the air, casting a shadow against the hot sun. All around it, people dressed in the black clothing of Mazda wandered around, some with law-books and some leading slaves around. There was no music or commerce, something very strange for a town. Perhaps, he thought to himself, it was best that way. Music is a distraction from studying the Law of Mazda, and from waging the holy war, bringing all the nations under the one god's thrall.

"Anakh!" a girl's voice cried out. "Anakh!"

He turned back to look at Astarthe, still luscious and beautiful, but she too had been forbidden from him. *If a man lie with his sister*, he said, *the sister shall be stoned.* Anakh had managed to keep their love-affair a secret. When he ignored her cries, he was protecting her. He left the dhow and walked onto the hot pavestone-covered ground.

Among the black robes of the crowd, great beasts towered above, and lawgiver warriors rode on them. The creatures, maybe five times the size of a horse, had scales like crocodiles, great beak-shaped heads and beady black eyes. Zayad Jabbar spoke from behind him: "A behemoth. To find their homeland, you would need to go east into the Desert of Hamma. But the desert will kill a man not accustomed to it. A deep well there is more precious to us than a diamond to a soft Fharese man."

The desert sounded treacherous indeed. "No water," Anakh

breathed. "I cannot imagine." At the thought he yearned for some. His throat had gone dry, and the burning sun did not help matters. The air wavered before him.

"There are worse things than thirst in the desert, though to a parched man he would not admit it," Zayad Jabbar uttered. "Sandstorms can come upon you suddenly, choke you to death if you aren't prepared. But in the Desert of Hamma, worse things come with the blowing sand. It whispers to you, boy. It tells you wicked things. The djinni who refuse to honor Mazda are there amid the shrieking wind, tempting you to forsake your vows, even as they bestow a curse of years, aging you five decades in the span of an hour. The sand destroys all. It brings cities to ruin, steals lives from innocent men. The sand is evil, Anakh. Do not go to the Hamma Desert without a guide."

Despite the heat, a chill ran up his spine. Still, he uttered the only word he could manage to think of. The sun beat unforgivingly upon them, heating the pavestones like a brick oven. From the tower, a singing voice rang out.

"Water," Anakh said, and imagined flowing rivers and lush oases. "Water…"

CHAPTER TWENTY-TWO:
THE WORLD BELOW

Weeks Before…

Claudian Adamantus the God, Monk Militant

Claudian had fallen many fathoms, from the lowest level of Cloud Temple Monastery to a maze of ice walls filled with a thick, numbing chill. His fellow brother in Hieronus, Luther, turned to him, having fallen just as far. Neither had injured themselves; as part of their training they had learned how to guard against a fall, even on the slippery ice floor. Luther balanced tenuously on his feet, fists at the ready.

Brother Luther is a better fighter than me, he thought, *but I must guard him against fear and clouded judgment.* "Luther, brother… be s-strong."

Luther turned to him, lips pursed in a solemn line, quite clearly forcing any fear to the recesses of his mind. "Brother, we must act quickly… shall we climb back up?"

Claudian shook his head. "No, brother. We have s-searched so long for what Brother S-Selmer found… now, we have found it, and we must go further."

Luther nodded. "As you wish, brother." He shut his eyes. "Hieronus, guard us against fear. Give us your justness of mind, purity of body, and fists of—"

A hiss rang out through the ice walls.

"—unerring judgment." He finished the sentence in a whimpering voice.

Claudian shut his eyes in response, and finished in a firm shout: "Help us to be living weapons in your Name." He opened them and nodded. "Follow me, Brother Luther. I will be with you all th-the way."

Luther gave a slight smile at the comforting words. He nodded. "I will follow you to the ends of the earth, brother. Now go, and lead."

~

Claudian led from the front through the rock-hard ice tunnels, managing to stay upright where any non-monk would have slipped a dozen times and broken bones. The chittering beyond the walls increased in noise and frequency, and Claudian knew for certain he was not alone. But he also knew he and Brother Luther were prepared. *A monk of the Order of St. Traber is always prepared,* he thought. Through his ceaseless training he'd honed his instincts; there was no strike of the dagger or blow of the axe he did not anticipate. He needed only a half-second to react. But still, he guarded against pride. Pride doomed you to failure.

The ice-wall opened up into a vault-like chamber. Claudian paused there, and Brother Luther's footsteps stopped at the same time. As he stood there, waiting for something to show its face, Brother Luther cried out.

Before a second passed Claudian had whipped around. Before Brother Luther lay the twitching corpse of an animal: if an insect, the largest of its kind, covered in a black carapace and bearing four quivering legs on its side. Its head, or what was left of it, had exploded, shattered by Luther's fist. Now, the hand of his fellow brother was covered in foamy green ichor. But the monster that had tried to kill him now lay in its death throes.

Luther turned, his face gone white. He shook the slime off his hand. "I did not see its face before I struck."

Claudian nodded. "You are s-strong, Luther, a living weapon in Hieronus' hand. Do not be afraid."

He turned and headed deeper into the ice dungeon, deeper to unravel the mystery of the Ancient Ones and the fate of the abbot Selmer. Luther claimed to see Brother Selmer leave the monastery while still alive. But more and more Claudian began to doubt. How could someone escape these monsters, this dungeon?

How can I escape? He shivered. But he would not turn back.

~

Claudian led them along through the cavernous ice tunnels, eyes always alert, heart racing despite his attempts to call it. In time he met one of the creatures face-to-face, staring it from down a crude ice corridor. More importantly he saw its face.

It had the body of a giant insect, like the creature Brother Luther had stricken dead. But its head—though bulbous like an insect—had the features of a skeletal white face, like a picture painted on a vase. Claudian's heart pounded faster than he ever remembered. He drew in a cold gasp. "Guard your mind, Luther," he whispered.

"You must be after the scrolls of prophecy," it chittered, in a strange language Claudian guessed every sentient creature could understand.

"Stand down," Claudian thundered back, without a trace of the fear he felt. "We killed your friend and we will do the s-same to you."

"You killed me," it chittered back, "and if you kill me again, I will live on. My mind lives in all of me. If you strike this body down, there will be another. There are too many of me to overcome."

Claudian drew back into the scorpion stance. *A wise monk waits.* Chittering echoed behind Luther. "I am a living weapon in Hieronus' hand."

"God-fearer," the creature chittered. "Before I changed, I killed men like you. It will be so good to kill a god-fearer again, after these many-hundred wretched years."

It darted at him, and in a second converged upon him, forelegs stabbing at him, but Claudian blocked hard and kicked with all his might, bursting the skull-like shred like a rotten egg. Milky green slime sprayed his face and the ice-walls. Seconds later, Luther struck the other with a death-blow, and whimpered.

"Let's go back," the weaker brother said.

Claudian crossed over, nearly slipping on the ice floors but managing to keep his balance. He held Luther in a tight embrace. "I am with you, and s-so is Hieronus. Follow me, brother. The god of justice would not lead us here if he did not have a purpose in mind."

Luther had gone completely white. Still, he nodded frigidly, and ducked his head reverently. He followed Claudian as he continued through the winding ice-dungeon.

~

The ice passageways ended abruptly in an immense vault a hundred yards wide. Set on a natural dais—a table of ice perhaps ten feet high—Claudian made out a giant rolled-up scroll. The ice ceiling was thin enough that the sunlight trickled through, and Luther dropped his torch. "The s-scrolls of prophecy," Claudian breathed. "This must be the reason why Hieronus brought us here."

"I don't know… there are… coincidences. Perhaps we should leave…"

"Quiet, brother," Claudian snapped, perhaps more harshly than necessary. Still, he needed to reign in his emotions. After decades as a monk, fear still had a hold on him. In battle, none could stand against Luther, not even a fully-armored knight, but against the ills and tumults of the mind he remained a sheep to the slaughter.

As they walked further into the giant ice vault, the chittering noises of the Ancient Ones increased in frequency and in volume. It spurred Claudian faster, but he could tell by the slow trudges Luther fell far behind, perhaps in overcaution.

Claudian bounded across the ice and leapt as high as he could in mid-run. He managed to catch hold of the edge of the dais, though the ice moistened and nearly caused his hands to slip. When common folk saw monks leap great heights, they thought they were gods, divine creatures sent from Heaven. But through a lifetime of asceticism, self-denial, and constant physical training, they had achieved the ability—though they became living weapons in service of their god, their power was not supernatural. It was not god-given, but earned.

At the top of the ten-foot dais lay a scroll in a writing he did not recognize. It lay there, rolled up and nearly a foot in length even so. But most tellingly, a skeleton lay there, and nearby it a torn-up monk's habit. *Brother Selmer never left.* Somehow Luther had been tricked: a device of the Ancient Ones, a phantasm sent to fool him, perhaps. He reached for the scroll of prophecy, whom these Ancient Ones or 'ancient one' was so determined to guard. And no sooner did his hand touch the vellum than three creatures came flying at him, having crossed the vault with impossible speed. He struck down two, smashing their heads with his fist and spraying himself with foamy ichor. The last one struck home, piercing his flesh with its obviously-poisoned leg. He answered the strike with a hard kick, sundering the creature's boneless head. He grabbed the scroll of prophecy and tucked it under his arm. At that the chittering reached a zenith: dozens of the creatures began darting out of the various tunnels that connected to the vault. Brother Luther fought alone amid a swarm of the foul things. Claudian would not bear it.

As the sea of Ancient Ones converged upon him, Claudian leapt, knowing he would never in a hundred years abandon the brother that he loved. He bounced across the creatures' foul heads like stepping stones as Brother Luther fought a losing battle and began to falter.

He grabbed Brother Luther but the Ancient Ones were massing, growing stronger in number as more and more poured out of the tunnels, scrambling all over each other. They jabbed at Claudian with their spiked legs, but now—prepared and aware of the threat—he dodged more easily, ducking and leaping out of the way.

Brother Luther responded to his grasping hand, heaving himself five feet in the air and landing on an ancient one's head. Together they leapt across the sea of monstrous things, cursed relics of ancient times, and made their way ever closer and closer toward the domed ice wall.

The Ancient Ones spoke in a chorus as the monks—fellow brothers under their father Hieronus—bounded across them, nimbly dodging each spearing leg. "You will die, pious god-fearers!" the thousands of voices chanted at once. It seemed all these creatures were one being, a shared collective mind. "Hundreds of years before your Empire began I lived well and strong. Once I was like you!"

It did not matter what happened to these Ancient Ones or why they or it was cursed. Claudian leapt for the wall and punched a handhold into the ice. Bit by bit he climbed the steeply arching dome, at any second ready to falter. The Ancient Ones did not follow; it seemed they could not climb. A quarter way up the ice wall, Claudian realized he climbed alone. He spared a glance down and there, among the swirling mass of insectoids, Brother Luther was pierced from back to chest with an ancient one's leg. "I am sorry..." Luther gargled. It was a wonder he could speak. "My fear has done me in."

Without a second's thought Claudian let himself drop, back into the hissing mass. He bounded across the hissing, buzzing hive, dodging each leg-strike as he swiftly made his way across the vault. "I will not leave you!" Claudian shouted.

Perhaps I do not have as firm control of mind as I believed. But it did not matter. He would not let this be his brother's tomb. Luther, his dearest friend, deserved infinitely better.

He tore his groaning brother from the monster's leg, and smashed the wicked creature's head with his heel. Then he began to climb—Luther and the scroll in one hand—and again, leaping two feet in the air, punching a handhold. Almost instantly he began to slip. This would be impossible, he thought. But it was worth it. He would not let Luther's body rest among these vile things. Ensuring that he didn't was worth the danger.

Bit by bit Claudian climbed, using his feet to their fullest capacity but going a tenth as fast as before.

"Long before your Empire took its infant breath, I sat in golden halls, the wealthiest man in Telantis!" the insectoids chanted in unison, a quickly-building chorus of voices. "I hid the scroll! I ate my brother for hunger! The Dark-Eyed Man promised me golden halls and wealth forever! And I shall claim it! *I shall claim it!*"

Chills spread up Claudian's neck, caused by far more than the ice wall he now struggled to climb. With his right hand now occupied, straining under the weight of the scrolls and his wounded brother—the brother he would not abandon to these vile things even at threat of his own life—he kicked and punched his way up the ice dome, slipping at each second, a single mistake threatening to undo all his progress, fall headlong into the hissing mass. The Ancient Ones, pouring in through the tunnels of the underworld, had become too numerous even for him.

At last, Claudian slipped too far. He stole in a cold breath, dangling by his left hand. Brother Luther fell from his straining hands into the mass. Claudian snatched the scroll as it fell, choosing the prophecy over his brother. He cried out, and knew he'd never be the same again.

As tears welled in his eyes he continued to climb, nimbler but staggered by the loss of his brother. Where the dome made its final curve to the roof, Claudian began to strike. He made a tunnel of his own like the Ancient Ones had, bit by bit, inch by inch, slowly making his way toward the surface.

A crack spread across the roof, a yard thick and a hundred yards wide. The roof was giving way. Claudian remained calm. But when he looked down at the hissing mass of Ancient Ones, they were climbing on top of each other, forming a pyramid of sorts and reaching ever higher and higher as they piled on. Claudian—if he escaped at all—had freed these monsters from their underground prison. As the roof groaned above him and the crack spread, he drew in a cold gasp.

At last the roof fell in, crumbling to shards of ice, and Claudian fell. For too long he dropped, landing at last on an Ancient One's head at the top of the mounting pile. He dodged two spiked legs as they speared him, then a flurry of a dozen more. He scanned the ground for a brief second to see if he could retrieve Luther's body, but glimpsed only a mass of swarming Ancient Ones, hungry for human flesh.

As more legs struck at him, Claudian drew his breath and jumped. His springing legs carried him ten feet in the air and ten feet across, long enough to land on the swirling snow in the shadow of Cloud Temple Monastery. The chittering of the Ancient Ones rose above even the shrieking wind and snow swirling around him. The peaks loomed above, and the great stone edifice of the Cloud Temple Monastery lay in sight. The sun was dipping below the horizon.

"Tell me, Hieronus, what sh-should I do?" Claudian cried out—the first time since his infant years as a monk that he prayed aloud—and the God of Justice and Just War's answer rang loud as a bell in his mind, though he did not want to believe it.

Flee! Flee from the evil mountain! You have recovered the scroll! There is no time to warn the initiates!

"No!" Claudian answered the Just God's words.

He sprinted toward Cloud Temple Monastery, and the Ancient Ones followed.

~

"Run!" Claudian screamed in the narrow corridors of the dormitory. "Wake up! Wake up! Arise! Run! Run for the lowlands!" He screamed until his lungs grew hoarse. The young monks in their habits leapt from their beds. The chittering of the Ancient Ones soon filled the halls and chambers of the monastery. *"Run! Run! Run!"*

As the hideous things broke into the dormitory, Claudian struck them hard, bursting their heads and breaking their spindly legs in his hands. Soon the initiates joined the fight, but they were not like Claudian, not as strong.

"Run!" Claudian screamed one last time, and struck his way down the dormitory halls, dodging the spearing legs and striking the insectoid's skull-liked heads. He could not win the battle against the Ancient Ones, products of a forgotten curse, but he could warn these

younglings—these greenhorn initiates he loved more than the Just God's command.

Though he had come back in to warn the initiates, he sprinted out alone. Scroll tucked underneath his arm, he charged into the evil night as the shadow grew. The moon did not show her face, and the stars were nowhere to be seen. *The night is evil. The night is dark.* But Claudian survived, and he had done the best he could.

CHAPTER TWENTY-THREE: THE WAGES OF MAZDA

Weeks Later...

Tiverio Lucullus, Maestro of Foreign Affairs

As Lucullus ascended back onto the High Plain, he was greeted with the dawn. It painted the yellow grass in a bronze color, casting its pinkish-red rays in a dazzling display. Though Valentus and his century stood guard over Lucullus, he could not help but feel naked and exposed. Not for the first time, he wondered if he should have stayed with the magus. He wondered if he should have gone with the padisha emperor to Taifun. Honor required it, perhaps. But he remembered Vera, sweet Vera's face, the young mother of his children. Perhaps, when he finally made his return to Imperial City, he would retire from the public service altogether. The pay was exemplary, but the risk too great. A farmer or tailor or tinker could not afford a luxurious apartment, but they had no fear of conspiracies or assassinations or doomed journeys such as this one.

The Southern World was in chaos, and if the Empire ignored these heathen followers of "Mazda," it would come back to harm them. That ancient fool Severus failed to see it, of course. Not for the first time, Lucullus wished Claudian Adamantus had stayed on the White Throne. Claudian was not a god like the Imperial Cultists of the east stated, but he had ruled infinitely better than the fool Severus. An ancient fool, Severus was, but a fool. Or something worse... a man who delighted in the destruction of Fharas, without seeing its long-term impact.

An hour passed, and smoke wafted up in the distance. Another burning farmstead, or another burning village. Lucullus ignored the distraction, ignored everything except his efforts to get home. But a line formed in the horizon, a black line of riders, swooping in from the distance.

"Shall we run?" Lucullus' statement was nearly a whimper. He clutched the reins of his horse so hard his fingers began to sweat.

"No," Valentus said, and his voice showed no sign of trembling. "They will outrun us. We must communicate with them, signore, or we must fight."

Lucullus did not know which one was worse. But the black-hooded horsemen came galloping in, throwing up clouds of dust, and Lucullus found himself praying. He prayed to Terrena, harvest goddess—the one who had served his family so well for countless centuries—though he knew there were better ones to pray to, and better things to do.

In an instant the black horsemen had surrounded him, and Lucullus stopped his prayers. The warriors had drawn out their scimitars and their faces—half-hidden in black cloth—had the look of bloodthirst. They did not want to keep him alive, nor give him mercy. Lucullus whitened and stiffened, and nearly slipped off his saddle.

"Enemies of Mazda, northerners all," one bellowed. "I am sent by the Most High Theomancer to put an end to your lives. You have intruded into the Theomancer's land…"

Fharas' land.

"…you have aided the heathen Pharzanes, a worshipper of many gods, a lover of images and eater of unclean things…"

Memories flashed back to Lucullus of history lessons… the Red Witch sitting on the White Throne, condemning all wine and statues and paintings.

"For it, the sentence is death. But in truth, the Theomancer has wanted you dead ever since you entered the land. He knew of your character far before then. It is said he can judge a man by merely looking into his eyes."

There were three dozen, he counted, less in number than his century. But their fighting skills, at least among the southrons, was legendary. In the Imperial tongue, he whispered to Valentus, "Charge them."

"Do not jabber in your unclean tongue—" He had barely finished his words before the Valentus and the century had attacked. Scimitar met shield; the sounds of shouting and clashing steel rang out across the wide plain.

The warriors of Mazda shouted in their own tongue—chants or religious phrases perhaps—and fought with such fiery eyes and angry faces, Lucullus hesitated before drawing out his sword and raising it high. "For Empire! For our country and its people!" Lucullus could not win a tavern fight let alone a battle, but he would do his best to provide some kind of support. "Kill these destroyers, these worthless creatures who brought only terror and ravaging to the world! The wages of Mazda is death, and now you must give them what they have brought to this holy land!"

He did not know where he was getting these words, but the black-garbed warriors—so unused to opposition, so unused to blasphemy—fought in a rage while Valentus and his men answered cool and collected, striking back with skill and levelheadedness in the Imperial way. One by one the warriors of Mazda fell to the piercing swords of the Imperials. At last, the captain—the one who had mocked them—whitened and turned around, galloping away on his black horse, terrified. In an instant, Valentus and the other men sheathed their swords and grabbed bows and arrows. A few shots later, the boastful warrior of Mazda fell from his horse, pierced thrice.

"Ride!" Lucullus snapped. "Ride all night and all day!"

After living under constant fear of the Dark Horde, nothing felt better than that victory.

~

Lucullus and the century rode from dawn to dusk unmolested, but despite the good fortune he could not help feeling—as darkness spread—that it was the last sunset he would ever see.

CHAPTER TWENTY-FOUR:
THE SUMMONS

Pyoter Matheris, Hunter

Pyoter sat at the table over a glass of wine, gazing around the main hall of the New Moon Inn. Thus far, in his midnight walks, he had not found any demon fetishes or anything that particularly stood out. But he had no doubts that the inquisitor had extracted the truth from that vile demoniac in Paladium… there were most certainly demoniacs operating here, and he was virtually certain that Barto Aldera was one of them.

The heavy-set, blond-haired man had a cold, reptilian look to his blue eyes, and the way he stared at Pyoter sent chills across his skin. That, in itself, did not convict him; but Pyoter had no doubts about it. He would need a small bit of proof, and then, whether by poison or threat, he would take Barto Aldera back for the torture of his life. The inquisitors would extract every last name from the vile demon-worshiper's lips, and then make a formal arrest, and execute them in the Magisterium or—more appropriately—in Imperial Square itself. This would not be a mere Hunting, a mere massacre of demoniacs; this, Pyoter had determined, would be a great lesson to everyone that taught what happened when you swore your life to shadow and joined the growing dark.

As he sipped his wine, Pyoter felt Barto Aldera's eyes on him. Even he, a seasoned Hunter, hated the feeling. *Nothing,* he thought, *would give me more relief than putting a bolt between his eyes.* But his crossbow lay in his room along with all his Hunting equipment, stowed away in an iron case with an adamant lock where none of these wicked demoniacs could find it and pry it open.

"Signore!" someone called from outside the tavern. Pyoter looked toward the open door; the bright daylight illuminated the form of a legionary. He breathed a sigh of relief. The serving wenches and the patrons of the New Moon Inn never failed to rack him with chills. "A word with you!" the legionary went on.

Pyoter nodded and stood up. Even with his head constantly facing the legionary, he could not help but see Barto Aldera's chilling smile.

~

"I do not mean to alarm you," the soldier said, his voice nearly drowned out by the noise of the streets, "but Emperor Severus has spoken with the Pontifex—deathly ill though he is—and he knew you were coming, Signor Matheris."

Pyoter nodded. His shoulders slumped; his muscles relaxed.

"He told me to say he has found what he calls a 'black book' with some names written in it... he would like you to come to the Imperial Palace. I am not certain what he means..."

Pyoter nodded. "Thank you, signore." All the stress of staying within the New Moon Tavern washed away with the soldier's words. The emperor had a black book which doubtlessly had the names of the demoniacs he was looking for; with Severus' help, he would arrest them, bring the wicked folk to justice, and return to the Pontifex with his mission accomplished, and time to spend on aiding his recovery. The Pontifex, after all, had fallen deathly ill.

~

With his iron-bound luggage in hand, Pyoter walked through the sunny day feeling none of the anxiety and uncertainty he'd felt in the morning. He said a prayer of thanksgiving to Hieronus Lord of Justice, as the soldier led him slowly but steadily down the winding stone-paved streets of Imperial City. Before an hour had passed, a road opened its way into the vastness of Imperial Square, with the giant white colonnades and domes of the Imperial Palace looming overhead. He had never been to Imperial Palace, of course, and the invitation was an honor beyond most any he'd been given. Now he would glimpse the lifestyle of the Empire's uppermost echelon and—though Pyoter found himself eager to get back to the Magisterium—he was eager to see the emperor Severus in the flesh.

Down immense arched corridors of unblemished white; past brilliantly-painted statues of gods, goddesses and national heroes; beside giant gold-framed pastoral paintings, Pyoter made his way toward the White Chamber. When he did, the immense White Throne stole Pyoter's breath; and the man who sat upon it was not who he expected.

Yes, it was Severus, but in Pyoter's imagination the ruler of the Empire was young, forty at most, with a stern nose, piercing eyes and a handsome visage. But Severus was old—frail, even, though he moved with great alacrity to greet him—with heavy wrinkles and a pallid complexion. Long white hair flowed below his shoulders, crowned with the glinting silver of the Imperial Circlet, and a longsword hung from his belt in a sheath. This, after all, was Bathalomer Severus, ruler of the six provinces, whom the Imperial Cult of the east called a living god. Seeing him, Pyoter was disappointed.

"Pyoter Matheris, Hunter, it is so good to see your face." The emperor smiled. He turned to the red-cloaked Imperial Guards flanking him. "We are discussing something very confidential. Please shut the doors and leave us."

The guards nodded and departed. When the doors shut behind them, Severus' ancient face twisted into a smile. "I have heard so much good about you, Signor Matheris," he said. "My friends in the Magisterium have nothing but excellence to report. I am sure you have heard… the Pontifex has taken deathly ill. I have done my best not to alarm the populace. I have not told them the whole truth."

"What do you mean?"

"The Pontifex has a disease, a terrible disease never seen before… he is covered in boils, wretched to behold… a saint in mind, but a monster, now, in body. I have good reason to suspect the illness is demonic in nature… that the thirteen cabals in Imperial City made a great sacrifice and cursed the Pontifex in unison."

"The heart of man is dark," Pyoter quoted. "Everyone who did that deserves to be burned alive… tortured… I cannot imagine sinking to such depths of evil. They deserve to be flayed!"

"They do," Severus intoned, "but so often people do not get what they deserve. So often the good folk suffer while the wicked prosper."

"I am unsure," Pyoter said. "In the end the wicked falter; somehow, someway, they get what is coming to them."

"I wish I believed that," Severus said. "You know why I called you, do you not? A black book with names…"

Pyoter nodded.

"It lists all the names of the demoniacs in Imperial City, all thirteen cabals. I did not want you to waste your time at the New Moon, when I have all that you need right here. Do not be afraid, signore."

"Why would I be afraid?"

"The nature of the thing, I suppose." Another smile touched Severus' gray lips. He turned and grabbed a book off one of the armrests. As he said, it had been bound in black leather—goatskin, perhaps, and a symbol of two snakes biting each other stretched across the cover—and when Severus tossed it Pyoter gasped, gone cold. He opened it, and there, dozens and dozens of names were written in blood, page after page, more—he realized—than a hundred.

One name he recognized—Barto Aldera, as he expected—but when he reached the last name in the book he gasped and half-dropped, half-threw it to the stone floor.

Out of his sheath, Emperor Severus had drawn a white crystal sword.

CHAPTER TWENTY-FIVE:
SCROLLS OF PROPHECY

Weeks Before…

Claudian Adamantus the God, Monk Militant

In the light of dawn, still shaken by the night's events, Claudian unraveled the scroll and found the ancient writing impossible to read. In his many hours spent at various libraries across the Empire, he had examined countless texts—writings of the Elders to the north, volumes of Khazidean myth, and ancient books of Eloesus that were old when Peregothius was in swaddling clothes—but he did not recognize this writing at all. Sitting on a rock at the edge of the mountain road, in the dead chill of a lonely dawn, Claudian knew it would take a miracle to understand it. He had serious doubts that the Empire's greatest scholar would even recognize the writing, let alone read it. Memories returned to him of the dread night in the caverns beneath Cloud Temple Monastery, a word used by the Ancient Ones—*Telantis*, a nation that existed before known human reckoning—and then he knew it truly would take a miracle to understand the scrolls of prophecy. But Claudian was a monk, a servant of Hieronus the Just God, and he had not yet undertaken his morning commune. Cross-legged on the rock, scroll of prophecy in his lap, he shut his eyes, and opened his mind to Heaven.

He had barely spoken the first words to Hieronus when a shock ran through him, and his eyes opened. The scroll shimmered with energy, and Claudian could read the words like they were Imperial script:

As it was, so shall it be again…
The King and God of Telantis, the Nation

Supreme above All Nations, shall abdicate the throne against the Will of Heaven. In his grievous error, shall he name a man King and God of Telantis unworthy of the Supreme Throne. And so then shall the unworthy man join with the Infernal Enemy, and with his dark brethren call a curse upon the Priest-King, and put upon him a dread disease. And if the King and God of Telantis does not avenge the Priest-King and slay the unworthy Pretender, then shall the Beings of Light in Highest Heaven destroy the nation of Telantis with fire from the earth, and turn the great nation into a great sea.

As it was, so shall it be again... Let the King and God of Telantis obey the demand of Heaven.

Just as he read it by the miracle of Heaven, Claudian understood by the light of Heaven. Somehow, his judgment had failed disastrously. Somehow, the emperor Severus had joined with demons, even cast a devilish disease upon the "priest-king"—the Pontifex—and if Claudian did not act quickly, the gods would destroy the Empire as they knew it. Telantis had failed, by the designs of the man who became the Ancient Ones, who hid the scroll underneath the ice and bore the punishment of the gods.

With the scroll tucked under his arm, Claudian leapt from his high perch on the rock, and barreled through the snow, descending the mountain in the midst of winter, sustained only by the training he spent his life to achieve, a perfect body, a living weapon in the hand of Hieronus.

CHAPTER TWENTY-SIX:
SURROUNDED

Weeks Later…

Tiverio Lucullus, Maestro of Foreign Affairs

By the time daylight broke, the black-garbed soldiers of Mazda encircled them in a giant ring. They were fast approaching, their black shapes growing in size, slowly forming into what they truly were: dark riders, destroyers of all life and joy, servants of an infernal god that brought only slavery and mourning to the peoples of the world. As tears formed in his eyes, a cold sickness formed in his belly, and he began to shake, he thanked Terrena that his century had defeated a few dozen of them, and he prayed to the harvest goddess that Vera would find a new husband, a husband that would not die in the line of duty, who would care for her and their children. "I love you, Vera," Lucullus whispered under his breath, and wished to the gods that she would hear him, a world away.

Soon the riders of Mazda lay within yards of them. All had drawn their scimitars.

One, riding a camel, rode ahead of the rest. "Heathen northerners. The god Mazda does not shed tears for your blood."

"Your god is wicked," Lucullus said, "if he is even a god at all."

"You will regret saying that, northerner," the leader snapped. "You killed one of our battalions. We have won against far greater odds. It must have been a punishment for their iniquity… perhaps they made an image, or perhaps they ate unclean food…"

"Or perhaps we were better," Lucullus suggested.

The leader's eyes narrowed. "I doubt it. But it does not matter what you heathens think. Your own king wants your head…"

"What?" Lucullus cried.

The leader laughed. "Ah, yes, Lucullus. He said you heard too much, and that is why he sent you on this death mission. You northerners are such faithless oath-breakers. Regardless, the Most High Theomancer has ignored the wishes of his friend and given you a second chance—"

"*Friend?*" Lucullus gasped.

"—and if you pledge your heart and soul and become a warrior in his name, forsake your heathen Empire and take up arms against the padisha and all the image-loving peoples…"

Lucullus drew his sword.

"If you utterly submit to the god Mazda and his earthly servant the Theomancer, then we shall spare you."

"I would rather die than join with your demon god! It is as Pharzanes said—Mazda has brought nothing but violence and destruction and oppression. I will never join your black faith."

"Nor I," Valentus said, calm and collected as he ever had been, sword and shield at the ready.

"Nor I!" cried a legionary.

"Nor I!" another said, and within a few seconds' time all had said the same.

The two lines converged, and Lucullus did not manage to strike a blow. But as he lay in the hot sun, in the midst of a growing pool of blood, he knew he had fought to his last breath, and that—in the end—was all that mattered. He uttered a prayer that Severus would be discovered, that his dark betrayal would be exposed for all to see; then he prayed again for Vera and their children, and fell into a dreamless sleep.

CHAPTER TWENTY-SEVEN:
ULTIMATE BETRAYAL

Pyoter Matheris, Hunter

In Pyoter's stunned silence, the demoniac emperor acted first. In an instant, he proved all the rumors about him. Sparks and forks of lightning crackled from his left hand and struck the white crystal sword in his right; as it collected energy, feeding off the electricity, the crystal sword glowed blue.

Pyoter fumbled with his case, fitting the key into the adamant lock with a trembling hand. At last it opened, but when he looked up Severus had the sword ready, once white but now burning blue. A smile crossed his ancient, wrinkled face, and for once it looked evil. The brilliance of the burning sword glinted blue in his old grey eyes.

"Have you heard, Pyoter Matheris, of Diogenus, the great Spellblade, that hero of ancient times?"

Pyoter did not respond; he had gone so cold, so rigid, he doubted he could shoot the crossbow.

"It is true I am a trained swordsman, but I am also a weaver of power," Severus said, the smile on his face widening. "It was terribly expensive for the Kheroans to craft an entire sword of *mooncrystal*, but I think it was worth it. Do you not agree? Diogenus the Spellblade, it is said, slew a dragon, even as I serve a dragon!"

"Why?" Pyoter said. "Why would the sovereign of the Empire serve a demon? I do not understand. You have everything…"

Severus cackled. "And even if I have everything in your eyes, I do not truly have everything. I am seventy-six, Signor Matheris. Ba'amut the Red Dragon has promised me an eternity in the world to come… and the world now…"

"So would the gods, if you'd let them…" Pyoter could barely speak.

Severus' cackle doubled in volume. "Ah, silly Signor Matheris.

At age seventy I lay on my deathbed in the Imperial Palace… in a dream the Red Dragon came to me, promised to save my life if I would pledge it to his service. And now, at age seventy-six, I still live. And I shall go on living. Know, Signor Matheris, that I am the maestro—as it were—of all the dread cabals in Imperial City. It is I who cast the demon pox upon the self-righteous Pontifex, with the aid of my lord Ba'amut. It is I that prolonged my life, and it I that shall reign as emperor eternal."

Pyoter pulled the trigger. The bolt shot toward him but a second before, a shape fell down from the walls: the body or corpse of a woman, pallid and smiling, dressed in the long pantaloons and buttoned vest of a comedic actor. Memories returned to Pyoter, of the cheery Yule evening that seemed so long ago now, the tall tale of the *Laughing Ghost.*

She giggled, despite the bolt protruding from her chest. "Ah, silly Pyoter," Severus said from behind. "You must realize you cannot win this battle. You may take the same path as this woman, who pledged her life to Log'ain the Betrayer and escaped imminent death."

Pyoter packed on another bolt, sidestepped, and pulled the trigger. This time Severus formed a shield of lightning with his left hand, sizzling away the bolt before it could strike him. Then he flexed his fingers and a lightning whip lashed him hard, burning him, stunning him, and stealing his breath.

Severus' cackling grew more pronounced, even as the so-called Laughing Ghost slunk back into the shadows of the ceiling. Pyoter knew this woman—whoever she was—had somehow made a transformation at the behest of these vile demoniacs. It was a thing unseen in recent times, recorded only in the earliest annals of the Magisterium… a creature of shadow, a veritable pawn in the hand of the demon that claimed her. A shadow of her former self, she now lay under the thrall of the demon prince Loghain: a powerful prince, Pyoter knew from his demonological studies, called 'the Betrayer' for reasons unknown. "Why?" Pyoter repeated when his breath returned, though he had come to realize he did not understand people half so well as he thought, that he had so terribly underestimated what mankind is capable of. "Why?" he breathed anyway. He dropped his crossbow; it would not serve him here.

"Oh, you simple-minded fool," Severus said in the tone of a cold, uncaring grandfather. "You should think before you speak. My task is clear; to kill you before anyone finds out. I do know, friend, that you will not put up a true challenge. Sometimes I wish I had a foe worthy of me… but those are too few." As a ball of sparking blue lightning grew in the palm of his left hand, a blue light glowed in his eyes. "To my lord Bahamut the Dragon Prince, the Eater of Worlds, let this wretch be a sacrifice to you. I will cut out his heart and lay it before your shrine; and in return I ask for another hundred years of life."

A chill suffused the room, colder than the iciest days of winter. The shadows throughout the White Chamber took shape. Pyoter grasped the hilt of his dagger, hanging from his belt in the sheath. *Protect me, Lord Hieronus,* he prayed though there was no saving him now. *Do not let me die in vain.*

He swept the dagger out and charged. Inches from a dagger blow, Severus hammered his lightning-blue sword onto Pyoter's shoulder, half-severing, half-burning his limb. Waves of electricity surged through his veins; blue lightning danced around his body, and the last thing he saw was Severus cackling madly, his visage turned to a mad old man, the ruler of the six provinces, the wicked grandfather of the Empire.

CHAPTER TWENTY-EIGHT:
LIGHTNING IN THE SKY

Claudian Adamantus the God, Monk Militant

By the time Claudian crossed the border into Anthania, the scent of spring filled the air, and summer came close at its heels. By the time he reached the outskirts of Imperial City, weeks later, summer had come in full. The sun burned hot on the pavestones, and the lack of water would drive the citizens to insane thirst, were it not for the aqueducts pumping gallon after gallon from the high mountain springs. The heat and poor quality of the air tempted Claudian to throw off his monk habit and lay bare his underclothes, but then, he knew, the folk along the main road would recognize their old emperor… at least, some would. But wearing the monk's habit, no one paid him any mind; to common travelers he was a mere ascetic, face hidden by a thin brown hood. Disguised, he was undetectable; and that is exactly what he needed.

The Arch of Conquest loomed high above him, and he passed under it, entering the city proper. Carved with reliefs of the ancient Anthanian War, it celebrated the first emperor Anthans, subduer of the indigenous barbarians, the Maritime Geats. From the Imperials' blood and the Geats' blood mixed together, a new race—the Anthanians—had emerged, and from it came the Adamanti. The Imperial historians had all said as much. His family, like many of the Knightly order, traced its origins to a mixture of peoples.

The noise—even in the heat of midday—assailed his ears even as the smells of spice, cooking foods, and refuse overpowered his nose. Then a pair of trumpets pealed. On the side of the street, a group of urchins in browns and grays scrambled off, sprinting toward the noise. Claudian realized then that the Imperial court had called a summons; and an announcement was on its way.

A sea of people had gathered around the High Podium by the time that Claudian reached Imperial Square. Severus, dressed in black and wearing the silver Imperial Circlet, approached from the steps of the palace, flanked by red-cloaked swordsmen of the Imperial Guard. At last, he took his place at the High Lectern, and began to shout. "People of the Empire, I bring to you news from the four winds! The Pontifex remains gripped with his horrid illness, but my physicians are attending to his every need so that he makes a proper recovery."

Claudian bit his lip. He wondered what a "proper recovery" meant to Severus.

"In the southlands, Fharas—the ancient foe of our Empire— threatens to collapse at any moment! Let us praise Imperium for striking her down! The wind of fortune blows at our backs, and soon, every people under sun and moon will call the Empire its master."

The crowd roared and clapped at his words, but Claudian did not join them.

"But not all news should bring a smile to our lips, dear citizens! There are, in fact, dark forces at work, even in our own streets! While you, the good folk of the Empire, go about your daily affairs, men and women among you have pledged their lives to demon princes of hell…"

A few in the crowd gasped; others scoffed. Claudian knew Severus spoke the truth, yet he was aligned with the growing shadow. It was a ruse to throw off suspicion, perhaps but Claudian did not know the workings of such a dark mind. And yet, looking at this wizened old man, he wondered if the scrolls of prophecy were mere fabrications or error-ridden fallacies, or worse—that the "miracle" of reading the unrecognizable symbols had merely been a delusion, a product of a panicked mind. *Ah*, he told himself, *I should not have so little faith*.

"My agents throughout Imperial City have discovered the names of most, if not all, of these vile demon-friends! The names will be published tomorrow, and they will doubtlessly shock you! There are respected priests, magistrates, even the high Augusts… and worst of all, the one you once called emperor, the very godsblood himself!"

Claudian went cold. *The truth comes out at last.* The fabricated names would condemn innocents to die. And his name would be among them. More than anything, Claudian realized he had to act now.

"Do not be alarmed!" Severus shouted. "The Empire will prevail against the servants of darkness! Our country will be a light unto all, a lamp to nations in the thrall of shadow."

Claudian shrunk back into the shadows of the alleyways and narrow streets, collecting his thoughts. Severus was old and frail, and, though younger than Claudian in years, decades older in body. He wondered how on earth Severus had secured this power, how he had kept his secret without any suspicion from the Pontifex. The frail, weak old man hid some secret, some powerful talent that he had never told to Claudian. "I sh-shall not underestimate him," he whispered to himself, and waited for night to fall.

No respectable citizen of Imperial City walked the streets after dark, and no sane citizen wandered the night streets alone. Thieves and muggers lay in wait, ready to pounce on the first easy target. In the public gardens throughout the city's wards, the degenerates—as some called them—imbibed Haroon spice and engaged in unseemly activity. So, too, did the brothels gain their best business in the night hours. No, there was nothing noble or wholesome about the Imperial City streets at night.

So why am I here? The answer was clear, though he felt like asking it. In the chill he made an ambling procession toward the Imperial Palace and the hill it rested on. With his name a target for the emperor's false justice, it was quite clear he needed to find his way in without detection. More so, to catch the emperor off guard. It was never good to underestimate a servant of shadow. *Above all, guard against pride,* he repeated the words of St. Traber in his mind. Yet when he had chosen Severus after abdicating, he had sensed nothing special about him save his intelligence and his now-disproven moral character.

"Hail! Signore!"

Claudian turned around.

A man stood there, cross-eyed, with the orange eyes of a spicer. A huge gap in his teeth glinted in the torchlight as he spoke further. "What's a man of the gods doing out here in the dead of night? Didn't your mother ever teach you not to go alone outside after dark?"

Two more shapes appeared behind him: a raven-haired woman with red eyes and—shorter than both of them—a ratling in gray clothing, his telltale whiskers sticking out of a hooded robe.

"For your own s-safety," Claudian said, "I would back off."

"A threat," the man continued. "No, your mother didn't teach you right about nothing."

"My mother was empress of the realm."

The man gasped and, for a second, seemed taken aback. Then he began to laugh. "Ah, right, your mother's the empress. Well, I'll tell you what, little monk, my mother's Issa, the lusty goddess of pleasure herself, and my father's bloody *Claudio Adamantus.*"

"Th-That is my father," Claudian stated.

"Enough!" the man snarled and had a run at him, striking with his dagger.

But Claudian, sensing the fight was not worth the trouble, shirked away and sprinted into the night, at a speed these common street thugs couldn't match.

~

An unknown, oft-overlooked security hazard to the Imperial Palace lay through a set of winding, forgotten alleyways. At the terminus, a stone wall was lower than the rest of the perimeter—a mere fifteen feet high—and the iron-grilled fence was a mere five feet above that. The smooth stone had practically no handholds, but with a tremendous leap and nimble fingers, he managed to grab hold of the flat surface and pull himself up to the iron grills at the top.

In his years as emperor—a time so far-removed and out-of-mind it seemed a century ago rather than decades—he had searched the entire perimeter of the Imperial Palace. He told no one. A flaw like that, a five-foot discrepancy in the wall, would deter anyone as much the twenty feet of stonework surrounding it. But with that small difference, a monk like Claudian could just barely overcome the obstacle. And soon, with another leap, hitting the stone-tiled ground without a sound, Claudian had breached the palace interior.

In the darkness, the giant building could nevertheless be clearly seen; the lights of candles and torches on sconces provided much dim illumination. Guards made their usual passes through the shady open spaces all around. But Claudian knew their habits. The penalty for intruding—a torturous, gruesome death in Imperial Square—deterred all common citizens for the length of Claudian's reign. As long as he acted quickly and quietly, the guards would not see him. The only true threats, of course, were the watchdogs.

Claudian darted across the way and leapt full-force toward a ledge. A dog began to bark, but he kept climbing. He would keep climbing until he reached an open window. Then he would make his way to the White Chamber, and execute the emperor with a strike of his hand.

A few minutes of climbing, and his hands brushed against a window ledge. He pulled himself up. No one ignorant of the Empire's monastic orders would believe it—an eighty-one-year-old man, scaling the walls of the Imperial Palace. But alas, it was true.

The smell of fragrant candles touched his nose. When he pulled himself up, the noise of two lovers echoed through the chamber: a red-haired woman with deep green eyes—Imperial judging by her aquiline nose—and a dark Eloesian with thick black hair. For a second the passions of the uninitiated rose up within him and he wondered, after all these decades, whether he had made a mistake, if— by swearing to celibacy and committing his body to the gods—he had taken away a font of joy. He would die childless, loveless…

"Hieronus help me," he muttered.

"*Get out!*" the woman screamed. "*What is the meaning of this? Get out! Get ou—*"

Spurred on by her words, Claudian fled their room, cursing himself for questioning the life he swore himself to more than sixty years ago. *I have not made a mistake,* he told himself as he dashed down the halls. Eighty-one was too old to question it.

~

Though he had not walked the halls in more than twenty years, and the torches on sconces provided only flickering, dim light, Claudian remembered every twist and turn. His years on the White Throne had been so relaxing compared to his rigorous training in Sanctum. There had been wine and hot food, conversation and best of all, travel. And temptation. Oh, had there been temptation.

Running through these ancient halls—even as alarms were likely raised all around him—he could not help but reminisce of the dark side of Imperial life. How many times did the maestros and maestras of the court say "Why do you do this to yourself?" or "What a torture!" They had no concept of why a man would dedicate himself to a monastic order, commit himself to asceticism, and foreswear marriage, family, and lust. And part of the reason he left was because after all the comments he heard, the forces of shadow had used them against him: a little voice told him to break the sacred vow, spurn his commitments to Hieronus and the serene Order of St. Traber, for temporal gain. How could the Just God forgive him after that? How could he forgive himself?

He ascended the next story, running faster than a dog in full sprint and—judging by the barks behind him—some were indeed testing that theory. Corridor by corridor he navigated his way until at last the giant double-doors of the White Chamber loomed above him. The emperor was likely sleeping. But the only way to the imperial bedchamber was here, through this door. "Hieronus guard me," Claudian prayed. "Let your just hands imbue m-my own."

He tried the door, and the iron hinges groaned. Saying another prayer, he heaved with all his might and at last it broke open.

Severus stood in front of the giant White Throne, a sword of crystal in his right hand. *He has been expecting me.*

~

"A pleasant surprise," Severus said, and laughed. He thrust his hand forward and the great doors slammed shut. "My predecessor, the one who gave me power, comes to wish me well."

"You know why I'm here."

Severus' smile grew. "Ah, Claudian Adamantus, I hear before your ascension to the White Throne, everyone thought you were a halfwit. How wrong they were… you ruled just as well as your father before you gave the throne to me—"

"Enough talk, S-Severus. You know why I am here."

"Why don't you tell me, instead of repeating those words? You're making me think your mother was right, that you are a halfwit."

My mother. A cheap blow. "Enough talk, S-Severus. You are a demoniac, a s-servant of the growing dark."

Severus laughed. "A harsh accusation toward your old friend, the one you personally appointed to the White Throne."

"Bathalomer S-Severus, I demand you abdicate the throne. I hereby place you under arrest. You will stand t-trial, or you will face immediate execution."

"Execution?" Severus said. "By whom? The stuttering halfwit?

"I heard your s-speech in Imperial S-Square. You mean t-to have me killed for the very s-sin you committed."

"Ah, you heard that." Severus chuckled. "A pity. I wanted to catch the demoniacs before they found out they were being hunted."

"Why?" Claudian stated. "Why, when you have everything?

Why, when you have the very throne itself? Why would you throw it all away, condemn yourself to Hell?"

Severus chuckled again, then pursed his lips in a narrow line. "You poor, sad dog. You believe everything the priests tell you, in the Book of Order or the Book of Love?"

Claudian had memorized practically every verse of the Book of Order. At Severus' words, his hands balled into fists. He had to strike fast and hard, but he had to stay careful.

"Being dead to magic and a halfwit, you never realized the power that runs through my veins, did you? I am a man of great power, greater than you—"

"Pride dooms a man to failure."

Severus laughed. "Ah, you silly, stuttering halfwit." He thrust his left hand forward and a spear of white-blue lightning burst from his fingers. Claudian, stunned, could scarcely breathe as Severus turned his attention to the crystal sword in his right hand, sending five jets of sizzling blue lightning into it and turning the once-useless weapon from white to blazing blue. "To my lord Bahamut the Dragon Prince, the Eater of Worlds, I give this sacrifice to you. In exchange for this stuttering halfwit's heart, grant me another ten years of life… He is not worth any more."

When Severus fired another coruscating spear of lightning at him, Claudian leapt out of its path, halfway across the room.

"The old stuttering fool is quick, but he is a fool nonetheless."

"I do not understand you, Severus," Claudian said. "There is not much to understand, I'd guess. You are, in all, a wicked man. You deserve to die; that much is all I need to know."

Severus fired a forked spear of lightning at him, but again Claudian leapt out of the way. "Die, you little rat, and spare the world your useless life," he snarled. "Your own mother thought you worthless. The very one who birthed you sent you off to a monastery so that she need not deal with you anymore."

He is trying to unravel me, make me act on emotion. He will not succeed. Still, it was strange to hear this man, the one he had called friend, the one whom he'd grown to like so well in the confines of the Imperial Court, act so wickedly. Twenty years ago, the old Maestro of Justice had done all the right things to earn his trust. For all Claudian's control of emotion, it seemed he could not judge people well. A terrible weakness for the ruler of the Empire to have, he mused.

He backed into the shadows, moving around without a sound.

"Hiding," Severus intoned. "When has that ever worked for you? Did you enjoy it when your mother hid you away? She was so embarrassed of you. Perhaps you enjoyed it when she hid you, so no one except a stodgy abbot heard your stutter or made secret comments about you when you were away... Ah, yes, my dear friend Claudian, people made many comments about you when you were gone. It must pain you to think about them."

Claudian no longer cared what he said. His mother had made a wrong choice but all mankind is imperfect, even Claudian. Though, looking at Severus, he remembered some were more imperfect than others. *It is time to strike,* he told himself, *but I must act wisely.*

A chill formed around him, a chill of both the body and the soul. He grabbed the holy symbol of Hieronus—a hammer, forged of blessed gold—from the folds of his robe, just as a dark presence began to drop from the ceiling. With a hiss, it retreated back into the shadows.

And a spear of lightning struck him as he dodged out of the way, burning him as he staggered backward. The cackling of Severus filled the hollow chamber. "The excitable folk of Imperial City call this shade the Laughing Ghost. Her true name is Malyrria. She betrayed her friends to save her life, and she got more than she bargained for... an ageless existence under the thrall of shadow, an eternal life of killing..."

"Eternal," Claudian said, and leapt across the room. Severus answered with another blast of lightning, but he was gone from its path. "...until Judgment." Claudian bounded toward him and nailed Severus in the chest with a flying kick. The scintillating blue sword clattered from his hand, spitting sparks.

When he brought his fists together to land another slamming blow, Severus was gone—more accurately, stumbling backward, and within seconds the magic-imbued sword lay in his hand again. Severus was wheezing as he staggered into darkness, the illumination of the blue sword spitting uneven light as he retreated behind the immense White Throne proper.

Claudian drew in his breath. For all his success, he could scarcely breathe; Severus had burned him badly, and his heartbeat felt erratic, uneven.

Behind him, the doors flew open. In its wake, ten members of the Imperial Guard stood there in their red half-cloaks and bearing swords. "What is the meaning of this?" one cried.

Claudian lowered his hood.

"Claudian Adamantus!" the same man shouted. "I thought you were in the north…"

"I came back when I realized th-the ruler of the Empire is a demon-worshipper!"

The Imperial Guard stood there, stunned. They did not argue; perhaps, deep down, it made sense to them.

Without sparing another word, Claudian had darted after the vile emperor Severus, the one he had called friend. He followed the flickering light behind the White Throne and through a corridor all the way to the very sky bridge, leading to the Council House proper.

Though younger, Severus ran a quarter the speed Claudian did. Not halfway across the sky bridge—a work of stone, dotted with giant windows—Severus turned around, realizing the error of attempting to outrun him.

Claudian's flying kick had quite obviously winded him. Drawing in raspy breaths, Severus nonetheless had the same fire in his eyes. He was still the angry, wicked grandfather of the Empire. And most importantly, he still had the scintillating blue sword, and the gleam of magic power twinkled in his left hand. "Stop, S-Severus. You will not win this battle."

The door to the Imperial Palace slammed shut behind him. Claudian did not spare a glance back. Severus began to laugh. "Ah, you worthless little stuttering halfwit. You are now a cornered rat," he rasped. "A final death-blow. The final challenge to my rule." He shot his left hand out and fired the bolts of electricity. The spears of pure energy tore into him, burning his heart and stealing his breath as he sprinted toward Severus. The entire sky bridge crackled with energy. Claudian's heart was ready to rupture when he launched into another flying kick.

Severus stopped the lightning and turned to run, but it caught him again and he slammed against the stone floor. As the last few sparks and lashes of electricity danced across the narrow walkway, Claudian's kick released Severus' latent energy. An explosion—half-electrical, half pure force—burst from his wounded body and sent Claudian flying backward, even as it sundered the stone and glass of the sky bridge, baring it to the elements. Severus' rasp had grown even more pronounced. Claudian ran at him. It was time to land the final blow.

The sky bridge heaved, ready to give way at any second. Inches from Severus, he ducked under and grabbed hold of him, then leapt onto the domed roof of the Council House even as the sky bridge stopped its shuddering. The ancient architecture would hold, for now.

The dome was so slanted even Claudian threatened to slip off and fall all those fathoms to his death. "I hold power over you, life and death, Emperor S-Severus, you wicked, wicked man."

"Lies!" he gargled.

"Tell me, for posterity, why you chose th-the path of evil and sh-shadow. Tell me why—"

"Silence, you stuttering half-wit!" the emperor hissed, still not realizing his plight, or perhaps too proud to admit it. "I will do what your mother and father didn't have the stomach for!"

Jets of lightning, more potent than any before, struck Claudian and sent him clambering behind. He fell, felt his body giving way toward the great drop, and his stomach churned. He calmed himself, ignoring Severus' poisonous words, and a half moment before the free-fall overtook him, managed to steady himself. But lightning burst from above, a sizzling-white, steaming beam of energy, which would surely have killed Claudian if he didn't leap higher onto the dome.

"The monks of St. Traber are masters of body and mind. I see that whoever instructed you in sorcery did not teach you the same."

"The one who taught me sorcery," Severus hissed, face-down on the dome and just barely clinging on, "could kill your worthless gods if given the chance."

Claudian paused, wondering if his words had any truth to them. He eyed the sky bridge, whose tunneled ceiling had been blown to pieces, and the Imperial Guard—as well as watchdogs and a number of roused sleepers—stood there, watching in awe.

Claudian leapt down and kept his footing, a feat that no ordinary untrained man could manage. He grabbed Severus by his thin, wrinkled hand and heaved him upward, even as he pitched his hand back and dealt him the strongest strike yet, breaking bone and sending teeth into the chill night air. A desperate scream of pain sounded from Severus' fractured face, and he fell. A last beam of lightning lashed Claudian, stunning him and sending his heart pounding, nearly knocking him off his balance.

As Severus fell, a shadow moved under him. No; a beast, for it had wings... it carried him southwards across the city lights, and Claudian could not tell if there was another rider on it.

Stunned, Claudian made his way down toward the sky bridge. He leapt onto the hard stone and fell onto his knees, feeling dazed and breathless, unable to control the movements of his body. Holes marred his brown monk's habit. Severus had dealt great, if not irrevocable, damage to him. He could scarcely breathe. *I have failed.* Severus had escaped. *I have failed.*

CHAPTER TWENTY-NINE:
A NEW EMPEROR

Claudian Adamantus the God, Monk Militant

There was no pomp to Claudian's quick coronation. As soon as he exited the sky bridge, laid bare as it was to the elements, the Imperial Guard raised their hands and hailed him.

"We will make another circlet, Signor Emperor," one said.

Claudian nodded wearily. His legs were still stiff like boards, and he could barely walk. More pertinently the White Throne did not seem a worthwhile goal. Yet—echoing the beliefs of his father—he had to consider the needs of the nation he led. His goal, immortalized in the dying words of his father, should be conquest; and his name should be Empire.

"Leave me, good s-signores. I have things to do. Know, signores, that I appreciate all you've d-done. Go, announce it t-to all the court…"

The main Imperial Guard inclined his head. Together, they left. When they shut the great double doors, Claudian felt his shoulders relax. His breathing grew deep and steady. He tried to calm himself, and though Severus' lightning lash had turned stiffened his muscles he managed to achieve the same calming meditative state he used to still his fears and ignore the concerns of the world around him.

He did not know how long he remained in that state, eyes shut, with no concerns for anything. It could have been an hour, but when he at last opened his eyes it seemed only a second had passed. And, in truth, Severus' wounds remained. Stiffly, he made his way toward the Imperial bedchamber where long ago, he had laid on sheets of silk and feather mattresses. Those years seemed impossibly far away, a different age from what he'd come to know.

~

In all major things, Severus had left things the way they were. The same royal blue sheets of silk lined the extent of the bed; the same wooden boards, lined in gold filigree, held up the structure. The same frescoes of ocean waves, sea-gods, and Imperial eagles ran the extent of the wall, and the same fragrant scent of burning resin filled the room, putting Claudian slightly more at ease. Besides Severus' personal belongings, all seemed well.

But beyond the near-identical appearance of the room, Claudian had a sense that something had truly changed. As soon as he entered the shrine to Imperium—or what once had been the shrine to Imperium—his fears proved true.

There, in the narrow alcove, Severus displayed his true character. An altar of chipped black stone stood against the wall, and above it, a miniature statue of a demon prince—a creature with large dragon-like wings, four arms, and a beard of tentacles—and chiseled underneath, the name BAHAMUT. Beside it lay a ritual knife.

There was more, Claudian realized, as he scanned the narrow space. A thin black rod leaned against the wall. Spikes surrounded the skull-shaped tip… if a mace, the poorest designed of all weapons. *No, Claudian thought, this is something else.* He grabbed it by the handle, feeling nothing but the chill of metal. Then, an instant, all changed.

~

He stood in a vast gray mist, a milky cloud of gray air. He saw no one, yet he knew full well he was not alone. A voice echoed all around, resounding through the vast space.

"Severus?" a voice said, thick and guttural as it struggled to speak the Imperial tongue. "Severus? No. Who is this?"

Claudian kept silent.

"Severus? No. Speak, dog! Impostor! Who is this?"

"Claudian Adamantus," he said firmly.

In his mind's eye, a face formed: an old man in a black turban, his mouth missing many teeth, with the gleam of magic or something worse in his left eye—for his right was covered with an eye-patch. "You presume to use this tool you know nothing about? Ah, you wretch. You will suffer for it. Where is Severus? *Where is Severus?*"

Claudian wanted to say he was dead, but lying—according to the Book of Order—never pleased the Just God. Instead, he kept silent.

"Fool! Dog! Where is Severus? *Where is Severus?*"

The black-turbaned man's left eye widened, and the strange gleam brightened. His sparse brown teeth bared into a snarl.

"Speak, dog! Where is he?"

Formless though the mist was, flickering and immaterial as the man's face appeared to Claudian, he slowly became aware of another presence, far darker and far greater than any of them, looming above and around them, watching. Claudian's blood froze and icy sweat formed on his skin at the thought of this dark Watcher.

He relinquished the mist and the rod he held, though he felt in that instant that the mysterious Watcher had looked into his mind and soul, and gleaned all the knowledge he desired.

~

Woken out of the strange dream, the black rod fell from Claudian's hand and struck the floor of what once had been the shrine. Hieronus' disapproval in him lay heavy around him, palpable. Claudian had used some dark tool, and somehow met a dark friend of Severus. A southron, quite obviously, for no one except the Fharese and the Khazidees wore turbans. Claudian fell back against the wall of the shrine, taking in cold breaths, the stiffness and soreness of his muscles growing harder than before. Worst of all, he realized that brief infinitesimal time with the rod had done something to him he did not like. He felt dirty, corrupted even. Watched.

Chills spread all over his body as he left the privacy of the shrine and entered the bedroom. He wondered if he would ever feel safe again. He shut the doors of his shrine and peeled off the burnt, pockmarked monk's habit. In his loins he climbed into bed, and laid the holy symbol of Hieronus over his chest. With the cold metal hammer resting against his bare chest, he no longer felt afraid. For the first time in many months and days—and despite the tools of darkness just a few steps away—Claudian had a good night's rest.

He slept deeply, and though his dreams were troubled, he did not remember them on waking.

CHAPTER THIRTY:
NEW ARRIVAL

Astarthe

Her brother had changed since the lawgivers captured them. They had turned him somehow, changed him from a loving brother and a servant of the Two Gods into a warrior, stern and unloving. They had hardened his heart, and worst of all, made him take the black. Each evening he practiced at the arrow range, even as Astarthe's looming doom came upon her. The Theomancer called her a sullied woman and said she was only fit to work in the harem. Astarthe could not think of anything she less wanted to do. She missed her brother's love. She missed her mother and father, Issachar, and the family she'd known. Each night she prayed to Issa the Moon Goddess and her husband Atman the Sun Lord, asking that they'd return her family to her… that they would put the fire of life back in Issachar's drowned body, and the spirit of love and goodness in Anakh's heart. But both tasks lay beyond even the gods in heaven, she thought as she wandered across the hard gray ground of the Theomancer's camp.

A behemoth let out a deafening squeal as she walked by; one of the lawgiver's calmed it. The midmorning sun beat hot on her neck; it was not even midday, and already sweat lined her skin. Mother Esma wanted her in the harem already for training. "If you don't please the Theomancer," she would say, "he will send you to die as a slave. Be glad your beauty has pleased him." But Astarthe could not be glad here, and she was a queen, who rightly deserved the Red Throne in Haroon. She should be more than this, a concubine to a vile foreigner, a lone strong woman in a land that had given up. In time she would give up; like a broken elephant, she would quit arguing with Mother Esma, quit resisting her sharp fingernails and sharper tongue, and resign herself to her fate. At the thought, tears welled in her eyes.

From the northwest a black shape grew in size, a shadowy

speck zipping toward them. Astarthe stopped and watched. Standing still, the beads of sweat grew on her skin and dampened her hair. Still, she had to see what was going on.

A creature landed on the baking gray ground—a winged creature with thick dark hide and a perhaps fifteen-foot span—and riding on him was a light-skinned northerner with bright white, shoulder-length hair and a wrinkled face. A sheathed sword, clipped to his belt, dangled halfway down the flying beast's back. On his head lay the Imperial Circlet, and she realized in an instant this was the northern emperor, the ancient foe of the Southern World.

Why in Varda is he here? she thought. *Perhaps he is after me. I should run.*

But she didn't. There was nothing worse than the Theomancer and his lawgivers, and she would much rather beg the northern emperor for her life than do the same with these folk, who did not allow women to speak.

The winged beast screeched and, in response, the northern emperor clambered off him. It took off once more to the sky, flying northeastward.

In an instant, lawgiver soldiers swarmed over him. They did not so much as touch the hilts of their scimitars or shout. Instead, they acted like friends. In the nomad tongue—the tongue Astarthe had come to understand—one asked, "Severus! Severus! What has taken you so far from the White Throne? We *need* you there."

The old emperor stood on his feet, staggering a bit perhaps from his old swollen joints. "I have been compromised," he growled. "The Adamanti have usurped the throne again."

Astarthe remembered Issachar's lessons by firelight, of Claudio-Valens Adamantus... Claudio the Destroyer, as he had called him, and spoken only ill of him. "Claudio the Destroyer stole the throne from you," Issachar once told her. "If it were not for him, the Throne of Haroon would be yours."

"A curse on his head!" a lawgiver snapped. "Mazda will destroy the dog in time. We will destroy the Empire, lay waste to all its images and idolatrous shrines—"

"Quiet," the emperor snapped. "I must speak to Umar. I have no doubt he is displeased, but he cannot be more displeased than me."

One of the lawgivers nodded and the emperor curtly turned and headed toward the Tower of the Theomancer. Often Astarthe wondered what was up there, what kinds of evil things went on, but she did not want to know. She hurried toward the harem, where Mother Esma was certainly angry at her absence. She tried to make sense of it all, of why the northern emperor was here and why in Varda he worked alongside the lawgivers. Most strangely, the name Adamantus, cursed by the very people Astarthe had come to hate.

Anakh

The barrens of Bajir were dusty and dry, and the hard-packed roads that ran along it took Anakh and his scouting party from one blackened ruin to another. The lawgivers had demolished a good many of the villages around here—those that wouldn't swear their allegiance to Mazda, and those that claimed to revere Mazda but kept crafting pictures and statues against his Law. Anakh, riding a horse with his fellow war-band, sometimes wondered whether this destruction was right. But Mazda and his lawgivers had given them a chance, after all, and they had spurned it. Anakh had as good as sworn himself to the faith, pledged to live by the High God's unchanging law, and had put on the black hood and clothing of his warriors. They'd taught him the art of archery, and by now he'd put all the idolatry and evil customs of the past behind him. Issachar, he was convinced, had gotten less than what he deserved. 'A man who dresses in garb of a woman shall be burned alive,' according to the Law of Mazda.

The noon sun baked the dry grass. The few trees—spread far out in such striking opposition to the rainy jungles he had known— whispered in the growing wind. They were ten miles outside of

Melchaddad in a sea of high yellow grass, and as they continued on, Anakh's horse nickered. "Calm, boy," he whispered, but Ekkar never had been afraid before, as far as Anakh remembered. The beast was trained for war, and his nervousness caused an unease to well up in Anakh's own gut. He nocked an arrow to his bowstring, just in case. Barach, leader of the party, turned back and scowled, muttered something about Anakh being "afraid like a woman."

Anakh bit his lip to stem a response. Barach was twice the warrior he was, and a fight would only end badly. In the hot sun he continued to ride Ekkar. He dreamed of reaching their destination, Bezakirah, and guzzling from its legendary deep wells, spending hours there long after they collected the monthly tribute. The Theomancer could wait before filling his coffers. The men were thirsty, and the burning sun had nearly put Anakh in a trance. Even now, riding Ekkar, he could feel himself nodding off.

An arrow stuck Barach in the throat. He could barely gargle as he fell from the saddle. Two more arrows zipped by; one struck Mahlil in the chest and another pierced Zair's throat. More arrows were launched and others died. *They are not attacking me,* Anakh realized. But why?

The culprits were hiding in the tall grass, wearing gold and sandy brown uniforms. Men of Fharas, he realized, looking at their trimmed beards. Even a woman crouched among them—married, judging by her veil—with a bow of her own. A woman warrior was against the Law of Mazda. Like Issachar, she deserved death.

"Anakh," one of the men said. "The brother-king of Haroon? The padisha will be glad to have you. Where is your sister?"

Anakh didn't know his Khazidean features were so obvious. "Astarthe is with the Theomancer, as she rightly belongs."

The man's eyes fixed on him uncertainly. "We will help you get her out of the Theomancer's camp…"

"I don't take help from lawbreakers. A curse on your padisha's head! May Mazda strike him dead. Praise Mazda!"

Anakh wheeled Ekkar around, steering him down the road.

No arrows answered his curse; the lawbreakers were as weak as they were vile. These assassins could not be tolerated; and he would tell the Theomancer personally. He uttered a prayer to Mazda, though no sacrifice lay within reach. He asked that the padisha be stricken dead, and that the Law of Mazda fall over all the world, and that the penalty for breaking it be death.

~

Back within the ash-gray walls of Melchaddad, in the shadow of the giant tower, the behemoths screeched at his coming. As he made his way toward the tower doors, they flew open and one of the Theomancer's servants stood there. "Come with me," he snarled, and Anakh could only guess the cause of his anger.

~

Up the winding steps of the Black Tower Anakh went, to places he never dreamed he would see. The Theomancer's dark-garbed servant led him up the stone steps, a torch in his black-gloved hand, illuminating the serpentine carvings that ran along the wall. As Anakh climbed higher and higher, the same unsettled feeling from before grew within him. He didn't know why, but it seemed the Theomancer was angry at him.

Then again, perhaps it's only his servant that is angry.

At the top level of the tower, the servant gestured toward the wall. No, a door, Anakh thought as he traced the thin outline with his hand. He pushed, and a draft hit him. Beyond lay a dim-lit chamber. He entered the Theomancer's private quarters, the most sacrosanct area in the city of Melchaddad where Anakh had only heard of great men entering: sultans and emirs from beyond, never a mere Khazidean refugee. He wondered what the Most High Theomancer sought of him, and more pertinently, if he wanted to know.

The secret door shut behind him, and he was alone.

Through a narrow corridor, Anakh navigated tenuously through the Theomancer's private chambers, having an irrational desire to turn and flee. He quieted himself, told himself not to worry, and pushed on.

The corridor opened wide into a grand circular chamber. In the center, on a pedestal, lay an immense orb of glass, its faint green glow illuminating the figure standing above: a man in a pitch black robe with a pitch black turban from which traces of gray hair poked out. A cloth patch of the same color covered his right eye, but his left more than made up for it. His gaze burned with intensity and intelligence. "Anakh. That is your name."

He was so stunned he forgot how to behave. Immediately he dropped to the floor, prostrate.

"You left your war-band to die. You retreated. You do know the punishment for retreating, do you not?"

Anakh drew in a cold breath. Footsteps echoed through the hollow chamber. *Someone else is here.*

"A deserter must be slain in accordance with the Law of Mazda. I have chosen to look past it—"

Anakh exhaled.

"—in one case. The good emperor Severus fled from his duties. I have spared him, for he still has great use to me. He has powers that may be used to great effect. But you, Anakh… as for you, I am not so certain."

Anakh went cold again. *I should have run.*

"Stand!" the Theomancer boomed, and Anakh clambered to his feet, barely able to breathe.

Standing in the glow of the giant orb, another man smiled at him: a light skinned northerner with white hair and a wrinkled face, and in his hands a crystal sword the same color as his hair. The smile he gave was not warm or friendly; it was the smile of a cat who'd caught a mouse.

Anakh took a step back.

"Run," the northern man said, "and I will fry you where you

stand."

Anakh froze.

"I sent agents throughout the Southern World. I asked them to bring you back, dead or alive, but preferably alive so I could arrange a triumphal procession. I would have loved to bring you back now on the wings of night, on the back of a fell steed, but now—*now*..." Silver glittered on the old man's head. He removed the circlet with his left hand and cast the priceless crown on the floor. "Now you are of no use to me. Or to my lord, the Most High Theomancer, who sees all."

Anakh's hand inched toward his quiver. The old man snarled and thrust his left hand forward; lightning cracked from his fingers, burned Anakh's skin and sent his heart up into his throat. He gasped and took a stiff step back.

"Insolent child," the old man hissed. "I should have expected as much from a Khazidee, a would-be king born from incest..."

The Theomancer was smiling. His black turban seemed to grow blacker; the air took on a heaviness. Anakh had made a terrible mistake joining these men, he realized. *Lord Atman, father,* he prayed, *preserve me.*

"What use are you to me?" the old man cackled. "Tell me, boy..."

Anakh's heart pounded out of control. He grabbed an arrow, knowing the pain that awaited him, and as the first cracks of electricity struck, he nocked it to the string and prepared to shoot.

But the electricity jolted him in positions he never meant to be. The arrow flew, missing wildly, and snapped in half on the metal wall. Anakh tried to run away but he only hit the floor as the lightning coursed through him. The cackling of the wicked emperor was the last sound he heard.

1093

CHAPTER THIRTY-ONE:
HARBINGER

Emperor Claudian Adamantus the God, Monk Militant

Claudian had barely sat on the White Throne three months, and already calamity after calamity piled up. Another rebellion, one messenger said, among the halflings of Kalamar. The insolent client king, Magon, struggling against the Empire's influence. The Pontifex, ill as ever and growing worse by the day. When servants came and said another messenger had come, this time from the Southern World, he nearly refused him entry. But Claudian—now eighty-two, yet still governing the nation that needed him—at last decided to hear him out.

The doors of the White Chamber soon opened, and in their wake stood a man. A huge gash marred his face, barely healed, and he walked with a limp. His clothing, though tattered, had clearly once been governmental attire. The faded remains of a purple sash dangled from his shoulders. He had barely entered the room before he fell prostrate.

Though the east and south considered him a god, he still felt uncomfortable with such acts of reverence. "Rise," he said.

The man grudgingly obeyed. *Gods, does he look wretched.* The scar had nearly disfigured him; it had the looks of a scimitar-wound. Tucked between his arms was a codex. "I bring you a report of the Southern World."

Claudian frowned. "And?"

"And Fharas is troubled. The King of Kings hides behind the walls of Taifun, not daring to leave." *It is a wonder he can speak, with that scar.* "I am Tiverio Lucullus, Maestro of Foreign Affairs, and I barely escaped with my life. Fharas has always been a thorn in the Empire's side, but the foe that troubles them is far worse than they ever were. They hate images and music and wine, everything that brings mankind joy."

Memories of his middle age, when the Red Witch arrived from the faraway seas, flashed back to him. Lidda, the supposed servant of the One, had nearly done in the Empire. She had killed his mother. At the thought, Claudian bared his teeth.

"Every people they touch, they destroy. They keep to their faith unswervingly but that is the only good that can be said of them. I am so glad Severus has been discovered; he is a snake, a poison serpent, and would not listen to me. He tried to have me killed…"

Claudian felt his eyes narrow. "Signore… what would you suggest I do?"

"My lord emperor, revered shepherd of our nation, I beg that you change the course of action we have taken for so long; I beg that you look no longer on Fharas as an enemy, but as an ally."

The proposition was bold; too bold, even for Claudian. "Signore, you have done well. Though I am certain you are right, there are concerns at home. We must focus our energies here, for now."

The man's shoulders visibly slumped. His disappointment nearly made Claudian rethink his choice, but it was the right course of action. These raiders, these outsiders, were doubtlessly a worse threat than Fharas had ever been; but it was not the Empire's concern until it became the Empire's concern.

"Your Undying Glory," the man continued, apparently unwilling to give up. "As you can see from my injury, I lay within inches of death. It is by the god's preservation that I am here today. I am certain they let me survive to tell you this; that the Dark Horde must be opposed, that the King of Kings and the emperor must join together."

Claudian stared at the wounded man for what seemed like minutes. His absolute certainty of what to do changed, in an instant, to doubt. "I will consider it, signore."

The man turned and left the way he had come.

~

As the afternoon wore on, the man's words only deepened his uncertainty. What if he spoke truly? What if the gods truly wished him to oppose these savages? But he was no longer a mere ascetic monk; his first concern had to be with the nation, the governing of the Empire, and leading it to prosperity.

At some point he found himself where—long ago—he had spent many nights and evening pondering great decisions. A vault in the lower levels of the Imperial Palace, lit in flickering torchlight, housed giant marble statues of national heroes. Here, in the lifeless stone gaze of King Anthans—depicted ten feet tall, sword in hand, with long hair flowing—he pondered his course of action. In view of Empress Irena—the circlet of command resting on her hair, and whom many outspoken women called the best ruler the nation had ever known—he eyed the sword she held, and wondered if she, now gone to the afterlife, would tell Claudian to join hands with their ancient foe. In view of Horatio, citizen-soldier—depicted perhaps eight-feet tall, shorter than the others, with the Imperial war-eagle standard clutched in his stone hands—he wondered if the ancient commoner hero would tell him to spurn ancient hatreds, put his father's policy of aggression to the side. Then, in view of King Peregothius, father of the Imperial race—a stone albatross perched on his shoulder, a stone beard nearly touching the tile floor, and on his head the bulky star-crown of the Sea Kings—Claudian fell to his knees, and began to commune.

The desire of Hieronus did not come instantly to mind. At times it seemed he did not care, and at times it seemed he wanted Claudian to act; at all times, his enmity toward this "Dark Horde" burned hot. Yet the words of the Just God hung heavy on him, and not the ones he wanted: *You must decide. You must act. You are the Shepherd of the People, and the Ruler of Six Provinces. Your duty is to command.*

So often the gods did not give him the answer and clear instructions he wanted. *So often, it is up to us.* He rose, staring at the eleven-foot statue of King Peregothius, and thought admiringly of the nation's founder. As a matter of principle the people hated kings, and that hatred formed the whole basis of the Imperial Council; yet Peregothius, despite his successors' failings, had deserved his power, and used it well.

Look out! the Just God commanded, and Claudian leapt halfway across the room.

The shade had fallen from the shadows, the one that Emperor Severus had created or, at least, controlled. She had the body-shape and the clothing of a woman, but her skin was paler than the whitest barbarian Claudian had ever seen; and her eyes had no human contours, black and dead as marbles. She smiled and giggled, but the malice she bore him was palpable. "'Claudian the Simple is back!' That is what they say around the palace. I hear everything, my pet!"

Like all wicked folk, Claudian knew this otherworldly shade delighted in attention. He turned and left the vault, though he couldn't shake the chill that consumed him. It would take an army of exorcists to purge this vile creation from the palace. It was not his concern now. Behind him, the shade giggled, and Claudian stopped himself from running, full-force away; that, after all, was exactly what she wanted.

~

"Your Undying Glory!" A man came sprinting up to him, wearing the purple sash of the Imperial Court around his shoulder. "Marco Benetus, Maestro of Justice." He had something in his hand, a black leather-bound book. He bowed. "I have found something Severus tried to hide. It has names…"

Claudian reached out his hand and Marco tossed him the book. The black-dyed goatskin tome had a snake insignia etched on the front. He opened to the first page, and there—on the yellow leafs of paper—were dozens and dozens of names, written in blood. A chill spread across his skin as he realized what this was. These names, some of whom—Lucello Bregantus, Captain of the Watch, foremost among them—he recognized, signified demoniacs. "Marco Benetus." Claudian kept his voice quiet. "Arrest everyone on this list."

Marco Benetus looked unsure.

"Do it. And scour their homes for evidence of demon-worship." On the last page, Claudian realized, was the name "Bathalomer Severus," confirming his suspicions.

Marco Benetus was looking at Claudian like he had lost his mind. "Signore…"

"*Do it,*" Claudian said, and placed the black book firmly in Marco's hands.

~

As his thoughts turned once more to Severus, he wondered where the wicked man had gone. He thought of the man's tools of sorcery, of the man in the black turban that had greeted him and asked for Severus.

The afternoon turned to dusk, and Claudian found himself outside in the crisp air, walking among the colossal statues of the Walk of Triumph. He found himself again in the presence of the heroes of the Empire. Small as an ant, he felt, kneeling before the twenty-foot statue of his father. Even amid the stone—worn, as it was, by rain and wind—Claudian recognized many of his features. The proud aquiline nose, the thick yet short-cut hair. But there were differences, too. The steel—or, rather, stone soldier's breastplate; the shortsword in his right hand and the shield in his left, which the Monks Militant of St. Traber foreswore; and the small cherubic creature on his right hand, swan-winged, with a hand of approval raised—the messenger of Fortune. So often he did not feel the legendary favor the gods had shown unto his father. They had blessed him for a purpose, of course, though the reason was not entirely clear and their work surely was not done.

Claudian bit his lip. "Father," he breathed, "what should I do?"

There was no reply from the giant effigy's stone mouth. Claudian half-smiled at the thought. Among the passersby a shout distinguished itself. He recognized it instantly as Lycano, a court servant, and turned to meet him.

Eventually the scrawny man found his way to Claudian, emperor, dressed plainly in a common monk's habit. Lycano wore his purple sash boldly, in the open, though such rich governmental attire would doubtlessly attract hatred from some. Inches from Claudian's ears, he whispered: "An emissary has arrived… he claims to come from the Southern World, but he does not look Fharese."

"Thank you, signore," Claudian breathed. As he made his way back toward the Imperial Palace, in the shadow of the giant statues of national heroes, he had a feeling this emissary was from the Dark Horde, and an even stronger feeling that—Monk Militant or no— eighty-two was too old to worry about such things.

~

In the White Chamber, the newly-forged Imperial Circlet resting on his hair, Claudian took his seat on the giant throne and examined the emissary. An untrimmed, unkempt gray beard fell halfway down his chest, contrasting starkly with his dark sunburnt skin. Over the thinning hair of his head he wore a turban of dark-brown cloth; and draped over his body, a coarse leathery material composed his robe, chewed as it was by fleas. Yet a scimitar dangled from his side, clipped to his belt, and his eyes contained a youthful strength. "Your Majesty," he struggled to say in the Imperial tongue, and inclined his head.

Claudian did not respond.

"I am a messenger of the Most High Theomancer, conqueror of the heathen Fharese. I come bringing goodwill toward your nation, in hopes that we may cooperate and continue trade."

Claudian kept silent.

"We have replaced their idolatry with the true faith of Mazda, and made his Law the law of the land. I understand we have been called many bad things by the ones we oppose. The Dark Horde, the destroyers; but we are not a horde but a disciplined fighting force, an army of god, and we destroy only the wickedness of those who came before. We call ourselves the lawgivers, for that is what we do; we bring the divine Law of Mazda to the world, for that is our call."

"What do you want?" Claudian snapped, already having lost patience.

The emissary's mouth opened in surprise. "We wish to begin former relations with our two nations; I wish to build a Temple of Mazda within Imperial City, and have you build a diplomatic outpost in Melchaddad. Perhaps one day, you will find the faith of Mazda and his law superior to your idolatry."

Claudian staved off a chuckle. "Tell your Theomancer this, Signor Emissary: His requests—all of them—are denied. No Temple of Mazda will be built in the Empire, nor will one ever be. I will not build a diplomatic outpost in the city of an enemy—for that, after all, is what you are—and I do not honor the existence of your nation. You lawgivers are my enemy; and the King of Kings of Fharas is my friend."

An Imperial Guard at his side gasped.

"Your odious law and demon god will never find a foothold in the Empire. Tell your leader the Theomancer that he is my enemy. Goodbye. May you come to ruin."

The emissary drew in a cold breath and fell back a step. But his sullen face soon hardened, and he swept his scimitar out of its sheath. The curved steel gleamed in the torchlight. A fearsome weapon, but one Claudian could overcome. "You have erred, heathen," he growled. "I have given you a chance to repent, but neither the Theomancer nor Mazda gives second chances."

"You are a fool, lawgiver," Claudian said. "A quick death is what you deserve, to brandish a weapon before the emperor. But I will leave you alive. I want the Theomancer to hear what I have told you. Tell him he and his demon god are my enemies, and the noble King of Kings is my friend."

The emissary snarled and turned around, then stalked off.

"Take his weapon and his turban," he told the two members

of the Imperial Guard that flanked him. "Shave his beard, and cut off all his hair. Then he will know how I feel."

"Your father shines in you," one said. The emissary ran off but the Imperial Guard obeyed their sovereign, wresting the scimitar from his hands, removing the turban, and shaving all the hair from his head.

CHAPTER THIRTY-TWO: HOME AGAIN

Tiverio Lucullus, Maestro of Foreign Affairs

Lucullus would never leave Vera's side again. In their quarters in Imperial Palace, they embraced for what seemed like hours. In his absence, she had given birth to the child they'd conceived; another daughter, whom she'd named after him—Tivera, nursing at her mother's breasts. Gaius and Marco, twin boys, both two years old now, clung to their father's leg and wouldn't let go. Their eldest, Bonna— just four years old—had thrown a tantrum of excitement for their father when he walked through the door. Vera, his wife, had been so worried that when he walked in the door, she nearly collapsed. But Tiverio Lucullus, head of their household, had returned badly wounded from the Southern World, and he would never leave again.

Over a meal of bread, slabs of pork, and deep goblets of red Korthian wine, Lucullus told his wife all that had gone on: of meeting the padisha emperor, of the betrayal of Severus and the invaders from the east, of the trouble that threatened to engulf the world as they knew it. "They killed the entire century and—I thought—me as well. But the Great Lord Mirza found me... his healers saved me. Even the Theomancer had thought I was dead."

"But he was wrong," Vera said, and at the words her blue eyes welled with tears.

Lucullus ran a hand through her reddish-brown hair. "And now, the good emperor Claudian knows just how vile the Theomancer is."

"And I know how brave you are."

Lucullus smiled. *I will never leave,* he thought. "I will never leave," he said, and put his hands on her shoulders. The children were fast asleep.

"No... no..." Vera said in the weak voice of someone who

did not truly want to resist. Her laughs turned to sighs of love as she fell to the floor.

I will never leave, Lucullus thought. *I will never leave.*

CHAPTER THIRTY-THREE:
EXECUTION

Emperor Claudian Adamantus the God, Monk Militant

From his perch on the High Podium, in the midst of Imperial Square, Claudian watched the demoniacs receive the punishment that was due. In all, about two-hundred and fifty people from all levels of society—from the most impoverished beggar to Lucello Bregantus, Captain of the Watch himself—stood there, bound in steel chains, and exhorting Claudian to grant them mercy. But he would not give mercy to those who honored shadow, who furthered along the growing dark. These wicked men and women cursed the Pontifex with a devilish fever. For efficiency's sake, the executioners would behead them, though they deserved burning or some other torturous demise.

A crowd had gathered in Imperial Square, some around the podium and others around the executioner's block. Claudian spoke loud enough for all to hear: "Know the punishment for demon-worship is death! If you worship at a demon-shrine, if you cast a curse on your neighbor or even your foe, using the powers of shadow… know that you will be found. It may be a month, or a year, or a decade, but one day, your dark secret will be exposed to the light of public knowledge, and from there only death and eternal fire awaits you!"

Claudian turned and left the High Podium toward the Imperial Palace, as the first cheers of the crowd met the blows of the executioners' swords. The Imperial Guard followed behind him, loyal soldiers in steel breastplates and red half-cloaks. He could not help feeling that worse troubles lay ahead, worse than these demoniacs, though surely they were the vilest refuse living.

~

Two months passed, and the first hints of spring arrived,

before news from the wider world confirmed his suspicions. A herald came from the deepest parts of Khazidea, that Claudian's humiliation of the emissary had sent the Theomancer into a wild incoherent rage. An army of thirty or forty or perhaps even fifty thousand was massing on the other side of the Desolation, and the garrison at Fort Tidus was severely unprepared. The lapse in time, Claudian knew, was so great that he could well have struck by now; and if he ravaged the grainfields of Khazidea the damage would be incalculable.

He summoned messengers—a dozen of them, in the vast spaces of the White Chamber—and addressed them in a firm voice: "Every legion of the interior must be summoned. All the legions of Eloesus and Inner Gad; all the legions stationed in Nichaeus; and every available soldier in Khazidea. We will put an end to the Dark Horde and call Fharas our ally."

~

Within three weeks' time, Claudian Adamantus—the venerable, eighty-two year old sovereign of the Empire—stood on alien soil, miles south of the red sandstone wonders of Haroon. An army of one-hundred thousand soldiers from across the Empire, a force of a size never seen before in living memory, departed down the Imperial road. Even on the firm, immovable pavestone, the journey would take twenty days at best. *I am too old for this*, Claudian thought, but regardless of it all, he would do anything for the nation he loved, the nation that deserved—by the gods' edict—to reign supreme.

CHAPTER THIRTY-FOUR:
THE DAUGHTER OF ISSA

Astarthe

Beyond the dead, dusty land, the one the northern peoples called the Desolation, was the land that Issachar—her father and mother from whose death she'd never recover—had promised her. The one that Claudio the Destroyer had stolen from her; but seeing this Theomancer and his co-conspirator the Emperor Severus, Astarthe wondered how bad he really could have been, in comparison. The lawgivers from all over their conquered lands had converged on this spot. The Theomancer had lifted the siege on Taifun. When the emissary, Essan, returned from his mission beardless and shaven, weaponless and without his turban, all the calculating sense the Theomancer had was replaced with rage. He had moved everything from Melchaddad into his camp and still he saw everything. Thus far Astarthe had managed to evade the Theomancer's attentions, though indeed she was, by their law, his concubine and slave. The *gleaming* did not work on him; the amulets and charms he wore perhaps had something to do with it. Others were not so protected, but as Issachar—bless his soul—had instructed her, she only used her power when absolutely necessary, and at all opportunities used her mind and cunning rather than supernatural means.

Thus, months after their captivity, Anakh her brother was the only man she had ever known—a miracle of Issa, certainly—but she had lost him too. She had managed to stay strong, though her family lay dead and it would be easy to give up, or fling herself off a high cliff; but that was not what Issachar or Anakh would want. If she gave up now, killed herself, that would mean her enemies had won; to kill oneself is to surrender, to capitulate to your enemies, and Issachar would want anything but that. With that in mind, she kept on, silently avoiding the Theomancer's attentions, waiting for whatever opportunity the Two Gods presented her. She prayed to her mother Issa ceaselessly, day and night, sleeping and dreaming, and perhaps that is why she still survived, or why she still had the strength to continue on.

But here she was, having descended from the golden rock-pinnacles and come in sight of the Khazan River, her birthright. Issachar had told her the river gave life wherever it touched, and green sprouted on either bank. But the land before her was only dry swirling dust and cracked earth. The northern people's word for it—the Desolation—was very accurate and appropriate. She could only imagine what lay beyond.

They pitched tents here, waiting—the Theomancer said—for reinforcements. It was dusk, and Astarthe stayed within the concubine tent with her fellow slaves. The Theomancer called himself celibate, though he had bedded most of his forty concubines, and even now, two of them had grown large with child. Others doubtlessly had his seed within them, and now it blossomed. The leader of the concubines, Mother Esma, did her best to comfort Astarthe. None of these beautiful women and girls wanted this life for themselves, but through experience and stories relayed to her, Astarthe heard that most women who rebelled against their lot were never heard from again. It was important to be wise; for if she did not survive, how could she accomplish the Two God's goal. Even now, in the Fertile Land where the souls of Issa's beloved children went after death, Astarthe knew Issachar watched her progress, asking their common mother to guide her. She wondered where Anakh's soul had gone, now that he betrayed her. She hoped despite it all, he too had gone to the Fertile Land.

The tent-flap opened, and the old light-skinned northerner staggered in. The white hair that crowned his head fell to his shoulders, and his skin had a wrinkled, ancient look that stood out starkly against the flames in his eyes. He was ancient, at death's door; yet Astarthe could not help but think he would live another hundred years, perhaps another thousand. Most forcefully of all, the air of magic power burst from him unchecked, and Astarthe stifled a gasp at the magnitude of his residual energy. Chills spread across her skin, and in an instant she closed herself off from the Font of power, trying to hide her own magic talent and avoid the man's notice. The deadness and emptiness that filled her gave her pause, but she refused to give herself away.

"Mazda has given me many gifts," the emperor announced, and the concubines talking became silent. All attention focused on him. "I am over seventy years old, yet my mind is keen and the fire of life burns strong."

Astarthe wondered if he truly thought anyone cared.

"The fire of life—when burning—must be transferred to another."

Astarthe recoiled, and wondered who the unlucky concubine would be. She said a prayer for her.

"The Theomancer has deigned to share his women with me."

His women. Astarthe felt her eyes narrow. *To him we are like cattle.*

"Who shall it be? Which lucky woman shall receive the life-fire of Bathalomer Severus, rightful Emperor of the Six Provinces?"

Astarthe scanned the room, seeing the concubines looking down, avoiding the man's gaze. When she glanced at him, his eyes—dark and cold, reptilian, seeming to look into a person's soul and see their darkest fears—met hers, and she cried out. *A mistake,* she realized.

"Afraid? Is the little girl afraid of me?" The old man laughed as he stepped toward her, and a smile drew across his wrinkled face, the smile of a predator. She drew in a cold breath. "I choose this one. I choose Astarthe."

Gooseflesh tore across her skin, and her heart pounded so heart her chest shook. *How does he know my name?*

"I once feared you would usurp the throne. I once sent assassins to hunt you down and remove the would-be queen of Haroon. But now I see what a futile exercise that was. I sense you do not have the ancient magic of the queens of Haroon—it skips generations at a time, I know—so you were not a threat. You are not dangerous. You are an innocent woman, a woman that needs an instructor in the art of love."

Astarthe nearly screamed, but of late she had trained herself not to show weakness. She backed away only a half inch before he was upon her, slamming her shoulders down to the fur floor of the tent. She struggled as he pinned her down, ran his tongue—oh, his slimy, wormlike tongue!—across her cheeks. He moaned as he prepared to force himself on her, and then, as he lathed her eye with his tongue, she screamed and drew on the Font of power, and in the same breath, forced herself into this Bathalomer's mind with all the strength of the *gleaming.*

What a cold, alien mind it was, calculating and self-serving to the core, but it had failed to resist her, and now it lay in her control. As Astarthe fell in a deep slumber, assuming control of Bathalomer and inhabiting him, she felt another mind within his—a dark presence overshadowing him, an entity that enslaved him even as it told him he was free. Despite the darkness of Bathalomer and his otherworldly master, Astarthe pushed on, controlling him like a puppet, and imagining gleefully what fate she would design for him.

CHAPTER THIRTY-FIVE:
THE BATTLE OF THE DESOLATION

Emperor Claudian Adamantus the God, Monk Militant

From Haroon—the northernmost tip of Khazidea, to where its life-giving river spread into a hundred fingers that bled into the Imperial Sea—Claudian led his army of one-hundred thousand legionaries south down the Imperial Road. An army this size would eat any lesser province dry, but Khazidea's productive fields provided ample food, and the water of the Khazan—coasted, though it was, by crocodiles and fiercer things—provided a constant source of refreshment and beauty. Claudian thought of his father, who had added Khazidea to the Empire's possessions, and wondered how—before him—the Empire had survived. When the King of Kings, now his ally, owned the lush fields of the Khazan, the yearly cost of grain must have been exorbitant. But the King of Kings had been deprived of this breadbasket, and perhaps that, Claudian thought, was the beginning of his troubles.

The folk of the Khazan River Valley were generous and polite, and though their customs were strange, their conduct made Claudian happy they'd become part of the Empire. The fields of grain, chickpeas, and watermelon passed them by. When they reached Fort Tidus, a square stone edifice, the Desolation came upon them suddenly, going from green to grayish-yellow dust.

The legate that stumbled out of the fort to greet them had the look of a man defeated. As Claudian peered into his eyes—Alesso Komenos, he remembered, a man of fifty years who had fought in these wispy sands back when the war between Fharas and the Empire had reached its peak—he said, "There you are!" and fell dead.

"Onward!" Claudian shouted. "Full haste!" The legate Alesso had fallen victim to some dark sorcery.

Marching at full-speed through the windswept Desolation, where faces and whispers showed themselves in the dust—the legendary malevolent ghosts that Khazidean storytellers spoke of—the taxing journey still took them most of the day. By the time they breached the swirling dust, and the high rocky land jutting above the horizon, the sun had near completed its day's journey. And at the edge of the Desolation, the army of the Dark Horde had assembled.

At first glance, the black-garbed warriors ahead seemed to equal their size. Worst of all, strange beasts—three or four times the size of horses—with hard bonelike features, a beak-like head, and taut, fatless scaly skin stood at the front with riders on their saddles. Behind the rank-and-file soldiers on horses or camels, bearing curved scimitars, Claudian made out a sea of archers at the ready. He was ready to charge when, from this vast sea of warriors, a man came walking out, an aging man with the same long gray beard and pitch-black turban he had seen in a vision, all those weeks and months ago.

"Claudian Adamantus," he said. "You have not used the rod I gave Severus for a long time; you have not met me on the gray plane or asked for my counsel. I miss our little talks."

"Where is Severus?" Claudian intoned with none of the false friendliness that this man used. If this man spoke with Severus as a friend, surely he would know where that winged shadow bore him off to.

"Severus is dead," he said. "The old man broke our customs, and we had no choice but to emasculate him and burn him alive."

"An Imperial citizen deserves better, even a snake like Severus."

The man's false smile vanished. "You shaved the beard of Essan against the Law of Mazda, humiliated him and sent him back with a damning message. I am glad this day has come, 'emperor.' Your people call you a god, the ultimate blasphemy. I will prove their error with great joy." He turned and walked back toward the army.

A lesser man would kill him now, Claudian thought to himself. *But the Adamanti fight with honor.*

As the sun set, the lines converged. Claudian fought at the front, snapping the necks of camels or desert horses then striking the riders with his adamantine fists. The spears of Imperials could drive back and slay the horse-mounted warriors with as much deadly efficiency as they ever had, but the steel spears could barely pierce an inch into the strange behemoths' bony bodies. Thus, as the last bit of twilight faded from the sky, and the stars once again showed themselves, the Imperial line began to falter, and the men began to lose faith. As arrows flew, piercing scores, and Claudian realized the most likely outcome—between the behemoths and the deadly arrows—was failure and slaughter, a faint wind blew at his back and an augur stood there, the Maestra of the Collegium, Silvana the Windborne, the winged cap fixed firmly on her lush blonde hair and the staff crossing her leather jerkin. Her blue eyes looked troubled, and it dawned on Claudian that he had not seen a single mote of their magic power. "There is something dark at work, my lord emperor. The whole collegium has tried to summon Wind, but there is something I've never seen before… an anti-magical ambience all around this army. Perhaps, if we were further away—Ah! *Look out*, signore!"

A behemoth was grunting as it charged him, its cart-sized, beak-like head pointed at Claudian as its blacked-robe rider guided him, barreling ahead. When it had come within inches, a half-second later, Claudian had leapt and landed on its hard, bony back. Its rider drew his dagger but an arrow from an Imperial soldier stuck him in the chest. He fell off limply as Claudian mounted the beast's neck, having no illusions of his ability to tame it, and began pounding its skull with his fists. Though he shattered bone and the beast screeched as it tried to buck him off, it did not die or collapse, only went wild. When Claudian—in between the behemoth's wild jerks of its head—caught sight of his army and the thousands and thousands of dead or dying, he despaired and imagined this Dark Horde enslaving the Empire, destroying his country like they had destroyed Fharas. Then fire came from the heavens.

As he continued bashing the behemoth's skull, he glanced

behind. Fireballs flew from the high rock behind the Dark Horde, and pillars of flame summoned from afar burnt entire battalions to ash. When the shouts of many thousands of riders resounded like thunder across the battlefield—cataphracts, he realized, he knew just what was going on, and more importantly, how it all would end.

~

When at last, the sun dawned over the Desolation, and the scorched bodies of tens of thousands of the Dark Horde lay strewn everywhere, the armies of Fharas and the legions of the Empire looked across from each other at the edge of the Desolation. In the proud eyes of the cataphracts, Claudian—weak and haggard from battle— saw no malice or ill will. When the litter of the padisha emperor came, carried aloft by his servants, Claudian walked out to meet him, and saw something he did not expect.

The history books lied—at least, they did now. There was no strange gold neck-brace nor nose-rings or earrings. He had his black hair cut short in the Imperial style, and no strange paint colored his face. The only opulent thing about him was his robe, dyed in all the colors of the rainbow. He was young, handsome, masculine in the Imperial sense. The servants sat him down, and he rose. Claudian did what would, until now, be unthinkable: he walked up to the padisha emperor, and the padisha emperor to him. Then he grabbed his right hand, and embraced him. The padisha emperor kissed his left, then right cheek.

"Friend," Claudian said.

"Friend," the padisha emperor answered. "And I have a gift for you."

Out of the ranks of the cataphracts and footsoldiers, a man who had the rich blue silk raiment and long steel sword of a Great Lord of Fharas, led a young woman by her hand. Her dewy, chestnut eyes reflected pure innocence, set in perfect proportions to her thin feminine nose. She had the copper skin of a Khazidee, but the beautiful features of a queen and an air of majesty. Below her swan-like neck, a silk dress—tattered and pocked with holes, though certainly at one time rich and opulent—covered her slight yet perfectly-curved form. At the sight of her, Claudian gasped and questioned all the vows of celibacy he had promised. He wanted this beautiful girl, though he was far too old and she most certainly did not want him.

His mind reverberated, as if with some kind of attack, but Claudian quickly regained his step—he had nearly fallen—and shook it off. "Who is this?" Claudian said.

"Astarthe, the would-be Queen of Haroon," the padisha emperor said. "I commend her to you, Claudian, for execution or imprisonment or whatever you devise."

"I will do none of those things," Claudian answered him, and the young Khazidee's face glowed with an exuberant smile. "She will come with me, back to Haroon."

"And there is something else before we leave, friend," the padisha emperor said.

~

Amid the charred remnants of the "Theomancer" and his tent, the men of Fharas led the way to his tools of sorcery. Among jet-black stones carved with runes, metal-lined skulls and similar bizarre objects, lay a giant orb of green glass. "This," the padisha emperor, Pharzanes, told him, "is how he saw everything. At first I thought I would have it, but wouldn't that be a far more incalculable risk? I wish to give it to you, lord emperor, so that these foul nomads can never recover it when they resurge."

"I will take it," Claudian said, though he did not want to when he remembered his conversation with the Theomancer in an otherworldly plane, and the third dark Presence that watched over them. At the thought, he shuddered, but he knew he had to, and ordered some legionaries to load it in a cart.

The young queen of Haroon watched him from afar with smitten eyes, and Claudian wondered how she could possibly want his love, when he was so old.

182

CHAPTER THIRTY-SIX:
THE EMPEROR'S LOVE

Astarthe

Behind the old man's aged features—though truthfully he did not look as old as he said he was—Astarthe saw the only mate she wanted. Thus, in the halls of the Red Palace, Claudian Adamantus the God spent the winter with her there. Amid the pointed arches and the lush garden courtyard, Astarthe made no secret of their love. The people—her people—did not need to know nor did they deserve to judge her. All that mattered for that season was her love. When spring neared, Claudian announced he would make her Queen of Haroon—though he forbade her to possess any soldiers, which in truth she did not care about—and then, inexplicably, the emperor monk died in her arms.

She mourned for days, but those days confirmed what she had suspected for weeks: the goddess Issa made her fertile, and she conceived. The emperor, Claudian Adamantus, was borne away on a ship toward his cremation and subsequent interment in Imperial City. Though her heart was shaken and she could barely think through all the tears, her coronation consoled her beyond all else.

In the Fertile Land, she could envision Issachar smiling, and her brother Anakh—wherever he had gone—pleased as well. She was queen. She had achieved the Red Throne of Haroon and through all the trials and travails she had accomplished her life's goal. As she grasped her swollen belly, rich with life, she looked out the red palace porch onto the clear blue sea, and said, "One day you will reign with me, Anakh," sensing it would be a son. Then, as the sun bathed her in his rich and joyful light, she said, "No… your name shall be Adamantion."

CHAPTER THIRTY-SEVEN: THE CHANGING FLAME

Pharzanes the Well-Born, the King of Kings, Padisha of Fharas

The peoples of Fharas once again clove together under one man. When he returned to Taifun, his subjects had greeted him with cheers and great feasting, declaring him the best padisha who ever lived. In his Taifun residence, he sent messages to all the loyal satraps with the list of names, to be publicized, of those magi and leaders who had defected, sentencing them to death. Then, quietly, he made his way to the Grand Fire Temple on the holy mountain.

~

The light of the Grand Brazier painted the face of Sidathra—newly-named archmagus—an appropriate red. In the crackling flame, he read signs and omens so intensely he did not realize his padisha stood there.

"Sidathra," Pharzanes said.

"Pharzanes," Sidathra muttered, and did not look up. "We have erred."

"What do you mean?"

"The northern empire has been our enemy. It always has been. It always will be. We should have let the nomads destroy them…"

"You jest," Pharzanes intoned. "Only with cooperation did we end the greatest scourge our kingdom has ever known."

"We did not end it," Sidathra said, still studying the flames. "The nomads have named another Theomancer. They do not have the power of the Orb any longer, but they are still nonetheless fierce. When we gain strength, we should fight the northern empire once again, and reclaim Khazidea. They were our enemy, and they should always be our enemy."

"I will not hear it," Pharzanes said and stormed off, though secretly he wondered if Sidathra was right, and if he even had the right to argue with what Athra God of Flame commanded.

CHAPTER THIRTY-EIGHT: THE VACANT THRONE

Lucius Arappo, Speaker of the Council

Lucius crossed the Sky Bridge that connected the Imperial Palace to the Council House. The tunnel that once shielded him from the elements had been blown off, now open to the wind and storm. How fitting, he thought, now that the nation was at a crisis. Claudian had died in the arms of his lover, the southron witch, and now the edict of the Adamanti had been broken. The citizens had spoken ominously of the lightning in the sky, what the councilors now knew as a battle between the wicked emperor Severus and the rightful ruler, Claudian. It was a fitting analogy of what was to come: an Empire unready to match the coming crisis, blown about by the wind.

EPILOGUE:
SHADOW AND FLAME

Thelimer Utheris, Priest of Hieronus and All the Gods, Pontifex

In his long and tortured, waking sleep, Thelimer had come to realize the emperor's servants had been poisoning him. Whenever someone came into his room, thinking he was sleeping, their faces had the look of skulls or dark mourners. Filled with pain and despair for many weeks, he at last renounced the Light and all its machinations, telling the dark spirits that if they healed him, he would serve them secretly, acting as the righteous Priest-King even as he covertly but earnestly spread the shadow all across the world. As soon as he did this—months after his hellish sickness began—his ailment was cured with his sudden death, and his spirit fell screaming into the netherworld with all the other spirits longsuffering in shadow and flame.

GLOSSARY

CURRENCY

Aes: A copper coin, the cheapest unit of currency. Also called a copper or an "eagle."

Denar: A silver coin, worth twelve aesa. Also called a silver or a "moon."

Liber: A gold coin, worth eighty denara or approximately one-thousand aesa. Also called a gold, a "crown," or a "sovereign."

TERMS

Adamant: A metal of light bluish color. Its existence was known, but it could not be shaped until the eleventh century, when the Alchemist Collegium created a flame hot enough. The process of making adamant weapons is so expensive that hardly any can afford one outside of the upper tier of the military.

Anthans: (1) Another name for Imperial City. (2) Anthans the Great, the last of the Sea Kings and the first emperor (having achieved the title with the ceding of Anthania).

Augusts: The higher of the two ruling classes (the other being Knights). They are the descendants of the original Peregothian families through the male line, and are the only people allowed to serve within the upper tier of the government.

Barbarians: A general term for non-Imperials, both to the north and to the south.

Desolation, the: An area of intense fighting between Fharas and the Empire on the southern part of Khazidea. The constant burning and leveling of towns has turned this once-fertile region into a desert.

Demons: The enemies of the gods.

Empire, the: A large nation surrounding the Imperial Sea. Their flag is a gold war-eagle on a red field.

Elders, the: According to legend, a race of mystical beings rumored to live "beyond the reach of the north wind."

Eloesus: An ancient land famed for its wealth and rich culture. Since the 500s YE, an Imperial province. Their flag is a laurel-wreath on a green field.

Fharas: An ancient empire centered in the plain of Gor Ilán. Their flag is a golden four-pointed star on a purple field.

Gad: The northernmost and least populous province of the Empire, known for its light-featured inhabitants.

Haroon Spice: An intoxicant, currently banned in the Empire, which causes hallucinations and feelings of euphoria but—over the long term—afflicting the consumer with severe weight loss and, oftentimes, dementia. Crimson eyes are the telltale sign of long-term addicts.

Hieronus: The god of justice and just war.

Hunters, Revered Order of: A secret order of warriors dedicated to rooting out demon-worshipers at the behest of the Pontifex. It has existed for about as long as the Magisterium itself has existed, but only recently became public knowledge.

Imperial City: Also called Anthans. The de facto capital of the Empire, and the largest city in the known world.

Imperial Council: A body of thirty Augusts (see above), given certain governmental powers, including the ability to remove the emperor. They are elected by the people of Imperial City across its thirty districts.

Imperial Cult: A group devoted to the worship of the emperors, especially the Adamanti, located in Imperiopoli.

Imperiopoli: A large city of Eloesus.

Imperium: The god of the Imperial state, represented as an eagle. His cult was founded in the 400s YE. The theologians of the Magisterium consider him a human invention.

Issa: Goddess of fertility. Worshiped mostly in Khazidea and the southlands, she nevertheless has a large temple in Imperiopoli.

Janshi: The capital of Sur.

Kernunnos: The wild god of forests, wildernesses, and changing seasons.

Korthos: An Eloesian metropolis.

Khazidea: A southern land along the Khazan River, surrounded by desert.

Knight: (1) A mounted warrior, especially one wearing heavy armor; (2) A member of the lower tier of the Imperial upper class—the other being Augusts—officially tasked with the defense of the Empire. In actuality, not all knights serve actively as soldiers.

Lorenus: The god of the sea, favored by the city of Peregoth.

Magisterium, the: A large religious complex in Sanctum, led by the Pontifex, chief priest of Hieronus.

Malleus: An honorary title given to full-ranked paladins.

Mazda: A god mostly unknown to the Imperials. His worshipers consider him the only good god.

Monk: A member of a religious order. Monks Militant go to war, but are generally forbidden to shed blood; some wield clubs or maces to overcome this barrier, while others are sworn to use their fists.

Path of Tidus: A long paved road running from Imperial City to Zarubad far to the north.

Peregoth: The founding city of the Empire, built on an island of the same name.

Spice: See Haroon spice.

Theomancer: The religious and political leader of all Mazda's worshippers.

Vestal: Generally, the Imperial equivalent of a nun in the north, a female monk.

Wall, the: A large wall separating the Empire from the northern barbarians. Its origins are a mystery.

White Synod, the: A council of seventy priests, with representatives from each branch of the Magisterium, headed by the Pontifex.

IMPERIAL CITY MAP KEY

Suburro: An ancient, poor section of town, flanked by the Equine and Aurean Hills. Though widely known for its poverty and shanty homes, many great Imperials found their origins here.

West Side: Arguably part of the Suburro, a poor section of town predominating much of the western two-thirds of the city. It is filled with parks and spice dens.

a.   **Armory District:** Once a center for the production of armaments and siege weaponry, this quiet district northeast of the Suburro is known for its charming shops and sprawling apartments.

b.   **Kings Terrace:** An ancient enclave near the center of the city, featuring the mansions and homes of rich councilors and government officials. Most of these mansions cannot be bought and are passed down through families.

c.   **Maxima:** Shops and theaters abound in this district, a center for drama and entertainment. Named for the war hero Adriano Maximus.

d.   **Villa Regis:** A wealthy section of town, built along the shores of the North River.

e.   **Bulus Wharf:** A section of town facing Imperial Harbor, a center of fishmongers and the fish trade.

f.   **Celsus Heights:** A rich section of town built on a steep promontory. It is named for the infamous shipping magnate Celsus, who — rumor has it — burned down the area to build one of his mansions. Beside the rumor for arson, he was known for his unscrupulous business practices, charging exorbitant rents for those who stayed in his apartments, and was rumored to be a Strig, a kind of undead. Today, the mostly sumptuous apartment buildings overlook Imperial Harbor. Shops and music halls can also be found in abundance.

Harbor District: A sprawling district bordering the Imperial Harbor, featuring docks and warehouses.

Cloaca: The sewer district of Imperial City, flushing effluent into the South River. In ancient days, the first Cloaca broke and gushed forth water into the low-lying fields south of the river, creating the Palladian Swamp. The second Cloaca was built, much larger and stronger, after years of construction.

g. **Market District:** A vast district predominating the center of the city, featuring its eponymous markets as well as slum areas.

h. **Canyon Row:** Shops, apartments, temples and shrines predominate this central section of town. The Walk of Triumph begins here.

i. **Newmarket:** A quiet district of shops and apartments.

j. **Mud Bottom:** A dilapidated, ancient section of town, the most impoverished district.

Avediccus: A section of town facing the Palladian Swamp. Predominated by homes, shops, and small shrines, a concrete stairway into the swamp can be found here.

k. **Meridia:** A section of town bordering the Palladian Swamp and city bounds, featuring apartment blocks, shops and administrative buildings.

l. **Mystia:** A large section of town featuring markets, shops and homes, as well as the garrison for the city watch.

m. **Villa Maris:** A section of town bordering the South River, highly developed, known for its taverns along the river's shore.

Emporia: Markets and shops predominate this central district.

n. **Loud Surf:** A section of town built along cliffs, featuring often more pleasant weather than the city below. Its inhabitants call this section of town the city's most blessed area.

o. **Perrine:** Named after the Emperor Perrius, this section of town has a mixture of wealth and poverty. It is a favored home for members of the military, as it connects to a road to Fort Mettius several miles away.

p. **Gaboline:** Named after the Emperor Gabolus, originally built around a fort then outside of city bounds, this district is known for its quaint stone streets and temples.

q. **West Limes:** A border area facing Wagontown Settlement, it is nonetheless highly developed and features vast theaters and gladiatorial arenas.

r. **East Limes:** A border area featuring many gladiatorial arenas. It abuts a section of cemeteries outside city bounds.

s. **Terrentian:** Named after the legate Terrentius, this section of town is known as a site of public executions. Shops and homes can be found here.

t. **Majorian Markets:** Named for two sprawling indoor market complexes, it is rumored that anything in Varda can be found here on sale.

The Ricci: A walled-off, closed section of town that houses the city's ratling population.

u. **The Strand:** A highly developed area of town known for its lighted roads, specialized taverns and bookshops.

v. **Mcletus:** A section of apartments, shops and temples bordering the North River.

w. **Urubus:** A vast section of town below Celsus Heights, relatively impoverished, where the smoke of the city often settles. City administrators consider it a public health nuisance.

About the Author

Cursed at birth with a wild imagination, Andrew Cooper spent his youth dreaming of worlds more exciting than Earth.

He is a graduate of the Odyssey Writing Workshop. His stories have appeared in Morpheus Tales, Fear and Trembling, Residential Aliens and Mindflights, among others.

Contact the Author

Visit **www.aj-cooper.com** to sign up for the newsletter and stay up-to-date on new releases.

Find him on Facebook at:

www.facebook.com/AJCooperauthor